VISIONS FROM THE DREAM GYRE

VISIONS
FROM THE
DREAM GYRE

short stories & poems
ANDY REYNOLDS

Published by Mosquito Publishing
ISBN-13: 978-0692846742
ISBN-10: 0692846743

Cover Art & Title Artwork by Brandon K Jenkins
(www.instagram.com/bkjenkins)

Poem on back cover by Andy Reynolds

Cover Layout by Mars
Author Photo by Mars

First Printing: 2019

the thief & the tree first published in the online magazine Th e Avant Guardian, 2009 (no longer exists)

Age of the Moth first published in the online magazine Thieves Jargon, 2009 (thievesjargon.com)

Dame of the Eagle Saloon first published in *Enflame: Esoterotica's 2nd Anthology,* by Sapiosexual 2014 (esoterotica.com)

For more on the writings of Andy Reynolds,
visit AndyReynolds.net

Andy Reynolds is also on Twitter, Instagram, Facebook & Youtube
@AndyWritings

It was at the edge of the world
I found her –
lavender twisted into her hair,
sitting on an old dock.

I joined her in the silence,
gazing out over the edge.

We watched the massive whirlpool,
a churning cone of idea & dream,
reverie & nightmare,
as it twisted & spat pieces of
dream into the air —
which we watched fly over
our heads like airplanes or gulls,
heading back towards the world
whence they came,
these visions from the dream gyre.

Table of Contents

Acknowledgments

An Introduction to the

Dream Gyre

I've always enjoyed reading and writing strange stories. As a kid, I was constantly sketching and was heavily influenced by surrealism. Now, as a writer, I am influenced by works of magical realism, mostly Haruki Murakami and Italo Calvino, though I do like a lot of dark fantasy as well.

That being said, some works contained in this book lean even more heavily into dream and experimentation than most of my other works do.

In 2008 I experimented with a short story process where I came up with a character and their life, and rather than write about them and their situation, I wrote a dream they had one night—basically telling their subconscious' interpretation of the events of their life and what they should do about it. Let's just call these "Dream Fragment Stories". I tried to let my subconscious kind of dream up their dream, and I attempted to create the feel of dreams in these stories by having situations and locations blur and change in the way they do in my own dreams. If it wasn't obvious to you yet, I'm a little weird.

Not all stories in this book are Dream Fragment Stories though.

I also write poetry and short stories for a biweekly show in New Orleans, called Esoterotica, where local writers read their original love poetry and erotica on stage. Some of the pieces in this book are works I've written for the stage of Esoterotica.

Other stories and poetry in this book are merely pieces I've written over the course of my life, with the oldest piece dating back about eighteen years.

For more on the individual pieces, there's a section at the end of this book entitled *Insight into each Story & Poem*, where I give a little extra information about each piece.

Now, for the obvious question about this book: What the heck does the title mean? What is a "gyre"?

A gyre is a gigantic vortex in the middle of an ocean. The vortex sucks debris into it—from shipwrecks, tsunamis, and such—and keeps that debris in the center of the ocean for a number of years before randomly spitting it out to wash up on distant shores. The idea of a gyre has been used in psychology for quite some time to explain how the mind can pull memories into it and keep them hidden for a while, but those memories may end up surfacing many years later.

When I came up with the idea for this dream-centered book, I was talking to my friend Corrinne Almeida, my main editor for my novel *The Axeboy's Blues* and my *The Agents Of* series. Before she even read any of the stories, she said, "Oh, your book should be called *Visions from the Dream Gyre*." And then she proceeded to explain what a gyre is, and the book was named.

It is my hope that these stories entertain and inspire, and certainly that they enrich your dreams, whether those dreams come to you while asleep or while awake.

VISIONS FROM THE DREAM GYRE

the thief & the tree

Gnarled and twisting with a reckless, unapologetic grace, the massive tree hunches there like a squatting giant with its enormous halo of branches. Not a trace of order lies in the twisting of its limbs—like hair so tangled, so knotted, that the only fix would be cutting it off and start from scratch.

He—*referring in this case to our hero*—looks up at the monstrosity, standing below in the thick mud, holding his lantern up in one hand to get a better look. Checking the straps that secure several odd-shaped pouches to his person, he attaches the lantern to a hook on his shoulder and begins to ascend the tree. This fellow is not by any means a climber by nature, but he does have very long limbs and fingers. With the occasional turning of his body to adjust the light coming from his shoulder, as well as the occasional slip of the foot or scrape of the hand, he manages to make it to the top of the tree, where the long, violet-colored flowers are blooming. The flowers, though smaller, are in the exact shapes of clarinets—green leaves twirl around them in places where the keys would be. There are thirty-some-odd flowers in total scattered across the top of the tree, and each is open and spouting out glowing yellow pollen and gray-blue symbols—each flower has its own distinct symbol that it spouts into the air when blooming.

Our hero makes his way slowly and carefully across the top of the tree, checking each flower he comes across, and half-way through them he finds the one he's searching for. He secures himself onto its branch with an extra strap, then pulls a large mason jar from one of his pouches. Setting the jar into the crook of two branches, from another pouch he removes a pair of tongs and a thin folding knife. Pulling the lantern around on his shoulder so that he has enough light, he holds the tongs in his teeth as he unfolds the knife. A gush of wind roars through the branches and leaves, pulling all the branches down and up again like a wave, and he hears the giant stir below him.

With the tongs in one hand and the knife in the other, he holds his breath. The flower's stem gives way to the knife as if it were made of nothing, and soon it is lying in the grip of the tongs. He gently places it into the mason jar. Putting the knife and tongs away, from another pouch he pulls a vial of blue liquid, which he pours into the jar so that it covers the cut of the stem. Then, after the vial and the mason jar are back in their respective pouches, our hero makes his way back down the tree—slower this time, since he can't rely on the lantern's light to see beneath him, and since he does not want to jolt the jar around any more than he has to. On his way down he passes another clarinet flower, spouting its pollen and symbols into the ether, a stream of I's and i's flowing into the air. He could have taken that one, he thinks. Perhaps he would come back for it later.

When he reaches the bottom of the branches, he hops down to the muddy ground and brushes himself off. At first, he thinks that the rumbling is the tree moving—uprooting itself and shaking the very ground —but then the rumblings become words and the tree is speaking.

I know who you are, it says.

Our hero shrugs. *I know who I am too.*

Why have you taken that flower?

Our hero opens the jar's pouch and pulls it out. The flower is there inside, full of life and spouting pollen into the jar, along with a string of G's and g's, the symbol that it manifests. *Because thin( )s will be more interestin( ) with this locked away for a while.*

Words are the river on which knowled( )e travels, the tree grumbles. *You cannot disrupt it without payin( ) a price. Many suffer when a train is derailed.*

Our hero shrugs. *Some words are ( )iven too much power. I'm just evenin( ) thin( )s out for a while. And words themselves are not knowled( ) e, but they are often treated as such.*

Your little trick won't keep people from believin( ), if believin( ) is what they wish to do.

You mean in ( )od? Our hero smirks. *He can be a bit odd, can't he?*

So that's what this is about, rumbles the tree. *Are you really so upset that you must seek to destroy him, even if it means destroyin( ) so many other thin( )s?*

Our hero shakes his head and slips the jar back into its pouch. *How many times have you been passed by, with people just ( )lancin( ) at you and sayin( ) 'what a nice tree that is'? You're just bundled up with the other trees they've seen, as well as all the ideas they've had about trees. But ( )et rid of the word 'tree', and then they can't throw a thou( )ht over you like a blanket—then they have no choice but to really* know *you, even if it's just for a few seconds.* Our hero unhooks the lantern from his shoulder, holding it up so that he can better see the tree. *I'm not out to destroy anythin( )—just to brin( ) some thin( )s into the li( )ht. To ( )ive them more substance.*

You won't destroy it? asks the tree. *You won't hurt my flower?*

I'll keep it safe, says our hero, patting the pouch that holds the jar. *I'll brin( ) it back. One day.*

Flowers

It was a small, white table—a modest addition to the tiny kitchen of my flat—upon which I was balancing myself when I first realized that someone else was in the apartment. I stopped fumbling with the rope and the ceiling fan as a man walked in. Short and broad and balding, he was dressed in a tweed suit.

"How'd you get in here?" I asked him.

"I broke the window and climbed in," answered the man. "You were making quite a ruckus yourself, so it seems my intrusion went unnoticed."

"I'm not sure what you're selling," I said, "but I must insist that you leave at once."

The man looked up at the noose hanging sloppily from the ceiling fan. "Indeed. But if I could just have a moment of your time, Mr. Lindey," he said, raising the briefcase hanging from one of his hands, "I assure you we can come to some sort of arrangement to your liking."

I looked down at him from atop the table and realized that for some reason I'd put on my best suit that morning. Since I was already dressed for business, and I had a feeling it would be more trouble than I cared to go through to get him to leave, I stepped down on to a chair, then to the floor.

"I suppose I may have another few minutes in me."

"Fantastic!"

*   *   *

We sat at the kitchen table and spoke for nearly half of an hour, after which time I packed a small suitcase and we went outside where a car was waiting to take us across town to the edge of the warehouse district. Most of the warehouses and factories we drove by were abandoned—sitting large, squat, and silent like giant metal boulders. Yet the building which was our destination took up a whole city block—ten stories tall, with smokestacks spearing the white clouds and spewing out large black pillows into the air. A tall fence wrapped around the building, and the man in the tweed suit nodded to a guard as a gate was opened for us to drive through.

When we walked inside, I could hardly believe what I was seeing—machines everywhere, all of them as big as rooms, with workers in greasy, dirty overalls walking, running, and hauling things this way and that. At a closer glance, I realized that all the machines were connected via a network of tubes, pulleys, gears, and chain. I looked around and was unable to find any amount of space where something wasn't sliding or spinning or rising up and down. Above me was an endless spiderweb of walkways, all weaving around machines which hung in the air above other machines, surrounded by countless chains and pipes and pistons—like an inverted castle of steel, copper, dials, and levers.

"You'll mostly be working in flora," yelled the man over the sounds of grinding and hissing and thumping as he led me towards the heart of the building. Beyond the clusters of machines and workers, there ahead of us was a cylindrical tower, rising from the floor up to the very ceiling. Lights bled from windows of the tower, and at every level several walkways emerged towards the rest of the building.

"We like our design teams to work directly with the other teams..." he folded his fingers together, simulating the teamliness he was trying to create, "...so that engineers and workers feel as essential to one another as they really are."

We entered the first floor of the tower and stepped into an elevator, across from which was a huge industrial elevator the size of a large room. The man shut the sliding gate and pulled two levers, and the elevator lifted us up through the tower. He tapped a gauge which displayed the numbers 1 through 9. "You're floor five."

There were three departments on floor five—Flora, Trees, and Fruit. Trees and Fruit took up most of the floor, with Flora only having three rooms: a design room with drawing boards, charts, and notes scattered about everywhere; a testing room, with test tubes, fabrics, inks, and chemicals; and a library, mostly filled with books about plants and their effects on history, culture, moods, etc. There was also a break room in the center which was connected to the elevators. It had a white table, a sink, and an icebox. The break room reminded me of my old kitchen, so I rarely used it.

*   *   *

I researched; I drew up plans and designs, then tested my theories; I deviated from used designs, blending old ways with new, and the months drifted into the sky along with the smoke from the smokestacks. I never got to know my fellow designers, and after a month or so they stopped trying to get to know me. They respected my ideas, and so did the workers —the workers liked how I kept them from making the same flowers day after day. The small group of designers got smaller and smaller as one by one they got transferred or promoted until I eventually worked day and night by myself.

I had a cot set up in the library, as well as a dresser for the few clothes that I owned. The length of rope from my old apartment was carefully coiled and sitting underneath my undergarments in one of the drawers. I ate mostly food that didn't have to be kept cold, so that I never went into the break room except to use the elevator.

I never accepted a promotion, at least not one that took me out of the department. Every few months they added something to my title— Manager/Executive Designer/Floral Specialist—all nonsense, but it was nonsense that was easily ignored.

One day I found myself sitting in the library with nothing to do. I'd read all of the books multiple times, I was months ahead of schedule and I'd drawn up all the ideas I had—even the far-fetched ones. There were a few chemicals and books I'd ordered that I was waiting on, but they wouldn't be delivered until the next day at the earliest. So I decided to do something I hadn't done for some time—I went for a walk.

Leaving the building's parking lot, I at once felt eerily like I was walking around in the past—like a stranger in my memories. Without the hum of my department rooms or the jumble of mechanical noise, the world seemed unnervingly quiet and empty. Empty of meaning, empty of hope— the bright blue sky taunting with its vividness up above. "You can never have this," it whispered to the people walking underneath it.

I walked through blocks and blocks of warehouses until I came to a small, quaint neighborhood. I tried walking through a park, but the flowers, trees, and grass bored me. So I went and sat at a trolley stop and watched the cars drive by. Some of them were bigger and stranger looking than I remembered, and I could tell that some were powered by different means than they used to be.

I heard a page turn, paper against paper, and I turned to see a woman reading on a neighboring trolley bench. She had long red hair and a bright blue dress. But her hair... it wasn't "red," not really. It wasn't magenta, nor apple nor raspberry nor blood nor... nor anything. It wasn't even a blend, it was a solid imperfection—a deviation. A mutation.

It occurred to me to wonder then—on all those floors of the factory, in all those departments, was there a group of people in charge of hair? Was this really an accident, a mutation? Or did someone purposely give this creature a head full of long, soft hair of such an indescribable color? And where did they find such a color in the first place? I became overwhelmed with my own thoughts, over-stimulated by the outdoors and the fresh air and this *color*. All the colors of the cars going by, the colors of houses and the plants and even the sky, paled away like some old photograph behind her—this girl quietly reading on a trolley bench.

She looked over at me and smiled. I smiled back—which probably looked weird since smiling in the company of others was not something I was accustomed to—and a trolley squealed to a stop in front of us. I followed her up the steps and sat behind her. Her hair spilled down over the top of the seat, and I looked around timidly, making sure that no one was paying attention. Then I took a pair of scissors from my coat pocket and cut off a lock of her hair. She glanced around at the *snip* sound, but I looked out the window, and she went back to reading.

I slipped the lock of hair into my vest pocket, where it sat above my loudly beating heart. I got off the trolley a few stops later, and then crossed the street and boarded another trolley going back the way I came, back to the park. Then I walked hastily towards work, feeling light-headed. My hands were sweating.

I took the elevator up to the fifth floor and walked into the laboratory. My hands were shaking and I had to take deep breaths to steady them. I pulled on a lab coat and goggles, then carefully pulled the hair from my vest pocket, slipped it into a test tube and put it over a burner.

Working carefully with my limited sample, I added only a few drops of one chemical at a time, then took samples from the test tube and looked at them through the micro-slide machine, which projected it up onto a large screen.

I worked with the theories I knew and even a few I'd only tested a handful of times until I had the right consistency of theory and innovation. I dipped my rubber-gloved finger in, then looked at the shimmering unnamed reddish color dripping down the glove, and it was *everything* to me in that moment.

I took the test tube and walked quickly out, over the metal catwalk, above and past hoards of cranking machinery. "Out of the way, please!" I said to my workers.

They parted and I looked down into the tub of fabric they were preparing. "More bleach!" I ordered, and one of the workers pulled a lever and bleach sloshed out of a pipe and into the tub. "Close the lid and spin it!"

The giant metal lid was clamped shut and the machine began whirring loudly. I walked over to the dying gun—which was essentially a large upside-down funnel ringed with glass tubes, each with a different color inside, and several accordion-like rubber tubes running into the top. I spun the device until I came to the empty glass tube, then opened the top and dumped the test tube into it.

"Bleaching's done," said one of the workers.

"Excellent," I said. "Put it into a mold."

"Which one, sir?"

"I don't know." I waved my hand absently in the air. "Daisy."

The workers went to the press and put hooks through the outer holes of the heavy iron mold, then a small crane was used to pick up the mold and carry it over to the wall, sliding it into the empty *CARNATION* slot. They took off the hooks and put them through the loops of the *DAISY* mold, then the crane swung it over to the press.

Once they'd screwed the tubes and hoses up to the press, they pumped the bleached fabric in. After that was done, they used the dying gun to pump green into the leaf and stem hoses, then yellow into the pollen hose. Then they hooked the dying gun up to the petal hose, and pumped the color I'd found into the mold.

"Never seen a daisy that color red before," said one of the workers.

I turned to him. "Is that the color red?" I asked, tapping the glass tube.

"Not exactly," he said.

"It's..." I said, getting very close to him, "...*not red*." I turned back to the machines. The process was complete. "Open the mold."

When they separated the two pieces, gasps came from several of them. Inside was a daisy—familiar, ordinary, yet at the same time new—a new sort of creature, a new sort of life which had never been seen until that moment. Something audible opened up inside each of us—as if a portal to a new and strange world was sitting there, broadcasting itself.

After several moments, I spoke: "Send it to the Dehydration Tank."

As if woken from their dreams, the workers began moving again—slowly at first, their memorized movements no longer coming as easily to them. Two of them came at the daisy from either side, with long tongs in each hand, and carefully picked up the delicate, moist creation. They brought it over to a towel, which they laid it on and slid it into the Drying Chamber, where the hot air gently dried the dye onto the cloth flower. Then they took it from there, put it in a large metal cradle which was suspended in the air by chains, and lowered it into the belly of the Dehydration Tank. They closed and clamped shut the dome lid and ran the machine. I clenched my teeth, and no one spoke. Somehow the whole factory of churning noise and cranking metal seemed to hold its breath.

Then a lever was pushed up and the machine came to a halt. A knob was turned and below the tank, on a small slide, a tiny object rattled down and stopped at the bottom. One of the workers used a pair of tweezers to pick up the tiny seed, and everyone looked at it in silence.

"Can you make more of the color?" asked one of the workers. "I don't think there's enough to make another."

"There only needs to be one," I said, not taking my eyes from the seed.

It was in that moment that I realized the city itself would be my new laboratory, and from then on I would walk through it, finding the undefined colors and hidden shades, every time making only enough for a single flower. Maybe it would spring up in a garden, or perhaps in a park somewhere, and someone would find it and it would change the way they perceived the world. Or perhaps it would just give them a moment's peace. Maybe it would grow in a forest or upon a mountain where no one would ever come across its beauty. But I would know. I and my workers would behold the deviant beauty before we sent it off to the Distribution Department, lost in a box of identical seeds, and that knowledge would be enough—it would satiate me—at least for now.

The Iris

Her eyes fluttered from the book like two darting butterflies—long, curved eyelashes in place of wings. Setting the book down on her lap, she looked about the cylindrical wooden room. Set into the curving wall of smooth, knotted wood were the Eleven Doors—each of them uniquely decorated and painted, each of them facing her from their place in the wall. Then she heard it again—a distinct *rapping*. Standing and setting the book down on the wicker chair, she turned to the Eleven Doors and crossed the smooth wooden floor which depicted the rings of a tree. It seemed so long ago that this tree had been hollowed out for her, and the Eleven Doors put in place.

She approached the fifth door—it was consumed in ivy except for the door's center, into which was etched a castle. Reaching into the ivy, she found the doorknob, onto which was painted a violet and aqua eye—for she was known as *The Iris* in the world beyond this door. As she turned the knob in her slender hand, the whole door clicked twice, then began tipping away from her like an oversized domino. The doorknob slipped from her grasp as the door fell, nothing waiting on the other side except for empty, still darkness. The door landed on the ground with a tremendous *clap*, where it opened up like a book, then opened yet again—trees and mountains folding out of it, then rocks, grass, and cliffs; oceans and cloud-filled skies; castles and villages all blooming out to fill each crevice of empty space until there was no space left to fill.

The Iris stood in the mouth of a vast cave set into a high cliff face, looking down upon the rivers, valleys, and kingdoms far below. In the distance, far beyond where the land ended, she saw in the vast ocean a slowly spinning vortex—the Dream Gyre. It had begun spitting out some of the dreams it had so carefully harvested. Had she been in the tree that long already?

Crumpled at her feet was a young man, broken and wheezing and bloody. His hair was long and deep red, his body weighed down by thick leather armor and chain mail. And when he looked up at her, she at once recognized his soft, brown eyes.

"Oh, it's you."

He turned away and coughed, his throat raw and destroyed. "Lady Iris." Blood leaked out from between the gaps in his armor, and she knew from his eyes that he did not recognize her. "I call to you, sing to you, beckon you to come to the aid of my people."

How long had it been since her place in existence was so severely and quickly altered? She wanted to speak to him, to make him remember—but he was calling to her in the ways of his world, playing his part, so she must go on and play her own role. She stood there wrapped in long strips of dyed-red leather, tied tight against her skin, the wind of that world whipping her long hair about as she peered down at this broken man.

"What offering have you brought to me?"

With obvious pain from each movement, the man pulled out a long object wrapped in white cloth and pushed himself to his knees, holding it out to her with it lying across both his arms. He bowed his head. "Lady Iris, I bring to you The Library."

She knew from the shape of the object that what he said was true. No one had managed to acquire it before, and she guessed that no one— including him—knew exactly what the object was or what it meant. She clenched her fists, wanting to ask him if he was sure, but asking questions such as that was not her place. So she reached down instead, pulling open the cloth, letting the open pieces drape down over his hands and arms as the dark-white light floated out into the air from the cloth, all shimmering like inverted, pulsing starlight. His body was shaking, but he kept his head bowed.

The Iris reached into the swirling light, letting it coat her fingers and hand like a glove as the light crawled like liquid up to her elbow. The light churned around her hand and arm like a whirlpool as she reached down to lift the man's chin, pulling it up so that he looked into her eyes. Small pieces of the light-glove tore away from her and circled his body, more and more of them until there were hundreds of lights circling him like fireflies. Yet he kept his eyes on hers, and she could feel him searching through his memories for her.

Then the rogue lights landed on him one by one, gripping onto his armor, clothes, and skin. He gritted his teeth and kept his eyes on hers as the lights on his flesh began biting down, tearing at the skin. Tears welled up in his reddening eyes as the orbs of light burrowed into the holes they'd made, swimming and pushing their way under his skin like so many little haloed bumps.

The Iris found herself almost pitying him.

His face finally contorted with pain, tears running down the chewed flesh of his face, his mouth erupting into a scream. One by one the lights traveled up the inside of his neck, over his jaw and cheeks, erupting from his eyes in the form of liquid light, spilling both down over his body and up over the top of his head. She held his uncomprehending gaze as everything the flowing light touched turned instantly sharp and jagged, hardening into something akin to crystal or glass. Short spires of crystal erupted from his cheekbones, chin, and jaw, his hair becoming long crystal icicles which bent and twisted the light that passed through them.

When the last of the stars had poured from his eyes, all that was left was a kneeling statue of jagged glass, staring up at her with worried, see-through eyes, its mouth open in a silent scream.

The Iris reached her arms behind her and stretched. The mouth of the cave and the rock walls grew larger around her as the glass statue too became enormous, and she took a step forward into the statue's open would-be-screaming mouth. She stood on his tongue, which was like standing on the wreckage of a glass house that had been shattered and then fused back together in its broken state. She looked down the cavern of his throat, which arched downward a few steps ahead. Yet nothing was dark, everything was lit by chaotically bent and refracted light.

With two fingers, The Iris reached into her mouth and dragged her nails along the inside of her cheek, pulling out a butterfly's wing, all golden and burgundy. Then she did the same to her other cheek, pulling out a second wing. When she put the two wings together they began flapping madly, lifting away from her into the air. She reached out and caught the wings, cupping them carefully in her hands, and as she slowly pulled her hands apart, the wings grew—and between the wings, an insect-body formed and sprouted legs. She kept growing the creature until its body was almost half her size. Then she swiftly grabbed it and flipped it over her head and behind her, its legs wrapping themselves around her ribs and shoulders and chest, attaching itself to her back.

She felt the creature flex and stretch along her spine, and she touched one of its legs reassuringly. Then she took two steps forward and leapt down into the cavern of crystal, letting it envelop her as the creature on her back beat its wings manically to slow their descent. The cave grew wider as she glided down the crystal tunnel, the light bending and shifting in strange, subtle ways—somehow warping the colors around her into leering, ominous versions of their former selves. Looking more closely, she watched as an innocent red bent and folded into itself over and over until it became obsessive and self-aggrandizing, suspicious of all the other colors and their motives—suspicious even of her as it watched her drift by. The Iris saw that it was similar with all the colors—within moments they were trapped in self-inflicted webs of conspiracy and illusory power struggles, wandering through the crystal palace all paranoid and on edge. She felt them watching her as she passed, the creature on her back gently humming against her as she slowly made her way down the prismic cavern.

From below, a floor of glass was rising up to meet her. She gently touched down, the surface smooth and cool against her bare feet. She looked at the man calmly watching her from atop a throne of broken glass. His skin was pale, his hair like water that had been dumped over his head and frozen.

The Iris reached up to her shoulder and stroked one of the creature's legs and it stopped beating its wings. She felt it taking deep, exhausted breaths, warm against the back of her neck.

The man's voice was cool and confident, echoing back and forth across the large, empty throne room as he spoke: "Not very subtle, the way you just barge in here."

The Iris noticed that the situation with the colors in the walls had escalated and that they were now on the brink of a civil war. One wrong interpretation could easily erupt into chaos and bloodshed. "It seems I've been called at a strange time," she said. "But the appropriate ceremonies were performed, the proper words uttered, even a lost artifact—"

The man jumped to his feet, his boots booming a single crack of thunder across the large room—his thin, crystalline armor swam with reflections of the twisted colors. "I've been searching for you. You thought you could play us like a pack of fools—an intruder in the midst of our humble society." He shook his head. "Using our resources like a parasite!"

Despite the harsh words he uttered, something small and forgotten fluttered in her chest as he roared towards her like a raging lion. There was no recognition in those blue eyes that rushed towards her—but that was the point of it all, wasn't it? If he'd recognized her from before the change, she may never have gotten this far, and things would be so much more complicated for both of them.

Just as he was about to collide with her, she twisted and turned to the side, letting him pass as she reached over to the back of his armor and grabbed the glass handle there, twisting it until it clicked. He fell to the ground but struggled back to his feet, turning to her as his armor opened like a hundred glass doors, completely exposing his thin, pale body.

He wavered on his feet as she turned to the rest of the room, her eyes watching over the looming colors which stalked the two of them like hyenas—the colors wouldn't dare make a move as long as she was watching. The Iris walked up to the man, all frail and naked behind his opened armor, then reached up to his chest and pressed on it with two fingers. It clicked open like a door, swinging open on two squeaking hinges. His shocked blue eyes looked down at the opening, at the clouds of swirling particles which now poured out from him. The man began to shake, and something inside her wanted to touch his shoulder, wanted to hold him, tell him it would be alright—but she wouldn't let herself lie to him.

He shook his head, clouds of dust beginning to trickle from his mouth, his glass-ice hair starting to melt and leak down his cheeks and chin. He looked around the throne room as if he hardly recognized where he was—then his blue eyes found hers and grew wide.

"Oh. It's you."

"It is I," said the Iris.

"You're not the intruder."

She shook her head. "No, I am not the intruder."

He glanced back down at the escaping particles. "Where have you been?"

"Exile. You exiled me." She hated the quiver that weaseled its way into her voice.

He looked at his hand, opening and closing it. "I don't think I can do this anymore…"

"I know."

He fell to his knees then, bowing his head as the clouds poured from his chest, dispersing into the air. "Will I die?"

"Painfully," she whispered. "And slow."

He looked up at her. "Kill me, please. Or exile me."

She shook her head. "No." Then she turned towards the throne. "We all have our part to play." As death crept ever closer to him, she could feel herself growing in strength.

She walked up to the throne, the cool glass floor against the bottoms of her feet, the warm creature still clasped onto her back, and as she reached out towards the throne, the throne also reached towards her, and when the two met their forms kissed like old friends. The eleven names she'd been given clattered to the ground like dropped pocket change, then sprouted into eleven newborn trees in a circle around her—all thin and supple—their roots reaching down and breaking through the glass floor. The looming colors slowly relaxed with the softening of the glass walls, becoming a few steps closer to their former selves. Some were too far gone though and would have to be killed.

So she stood there in the midst of the growing trees, not yet taking her seat on the throne, her eyes continuously scanning the colors around her. She would wait and watch, for she sensed that the first of the aberrant colors was about to make its move.

Elven Creature

Betwixt the midnight hours,
the moon leans back
into a gibbous wane—
the Great River turns to ink,
reflecting in itself the Nowhere Bridge,
stretching out—
a line of bonfires in the dark.

You lean to me,
pull pictures from your lips
and push them
to my forehead,

your ears pulled sharp
into elven hooks,
eyes laughing green & silver,
the wind pulling your coat of whispers
all long & thin.

My lips lean into yours,
the space between worlds
thin & breaking,
our gravity drawing waves
from the ink water,
waves which crash upon the rocks below.

Your fedora falls back—
fire hair spilling onto my face and neck,
licking my flesh to life.

Tie your string of stories 'round my throat,
pull me into you.
I am broken,
so have no fear of breaking me.

The moon drips down the sky
in phosphorescent streams,
becomes our blanket
as I crawl atop you,
clawing at your clothes
until they become
a flock of ravens,
picking me clean
of all but skin,
then flying away.

You pull open my heart like a paper crane,
licking at the insides,
careful not to disturb the contents.
We orbit each other in slow
falling spirals.

I suck on your hidden language
as you pull stars
from my fingertips with
your teeth,
nails scraping slow
down the backs of my hands.

Thighs squeezing my leg,
drawing me tighter against you,
our hips like lovers,
as you coax moans from my mouth
like a string of apples,
squeezing each one in your fist—
letting the juice run down your arm
and body,
until we both fall into
elated exhaustion.

Then you curl into my chest
all still,
our bodies aglow

in the moon's warmth,
our dreams lapping at each other
like new creatures.

We don't wake 'til the bells of the moon
begin to toll.

Already you are fading,
seeping back into your own kingdom,
the bonfires of the Nowhere Bridge sputtering out behind you,
one by one,
and you make your leave.

Compass & Ion

Beautiful nothingness reigned for eternity—nothing but quiet, humming silence and bliss. But eternity only lasts forever when you're there—once you're out, maybe it's been five days, maybe five years.

First, there were noises at the edge of that eternity—small, indistinct creatures jumping in and out of existence. Next came the sense of the universe being bound, constricted. The constrictions tightened, pulling existence into a shape—at each tightening the noises became more particular, molding into actual *voices* that were communicating with each other.

"Alright," said one of them. "We've almost got it."

"You said that last time," said another voice.

"Shut up and help me pull one more time! She's almost there!"

"I can't! The straps are cutting into my hands and they won't go any tighter! You aren't even pulling, are you?"

"Dig your boot into her back and pull the bloody straps, boy!"

The constriction tightened once more—the boundaries around existence taking the form of flesh as a tidal wave of memory and identity flooded through the skin like blood.

Two eyes opened to a burning world of light and color, a mouth gasping for air, a body aching with the pain of existence. She rolled over and fell off of a platform, landing hard on a wooden floor.

"I told ya not to let her fall!" yelled a voice.

Pain seared through her arm. She rolled onto her back and sat up, holding her arm and looking around at the treetops all around, at the large platform she was on. There were other platforms as far as she could see, floating islands among the trees with rope bridges, pulleys, and ladders linking them all together like a spider's web, though they were all empty. Next to her sat the wooden table she'd been lying on. *The strapping table*, she remembered it being called. A small square was cut out of the table so that someone underneath could tighten the straps of whoever was lying on top. She looked down at all the brown and black straps criss-crossing her body, knowing without counting that there were thirty-three of them—she felt the cold metal of the buckles against the skin of her back, legs and arms.

From under the table peeked a familiar face; young, green-eyed, and scraggly-haired. "Sorry I let you fall, Zeph," he said.

She reached over and ruffled his hair. "S'alright, Mikha. Your hands OK?"

He opened them palm-up, revealing shallow cuts in the dirty skin. "They'll be fine."

"Oh, don't go encouraging him now, Zephyr!" grumbled a voice.

She looked over at the old, overweight frog jumping off the table and onto the floor of wooden planks. He pushed a brass and leather contraption of lenses up onto his forehead with one slimy, webbed hand and held a candy bar nearly half his size in the other. "He doesn't take anything seriously!" His large yellow eyes were intense if a bit faded in his old age. He turned and eyed Mikha with complete disdain. "Never going to get his hands on a Compass the way he acts, not this one."

Mikha bowed his head. "Sorry, Sebastian."

Zephyr cleared her throat and Sebastian turned to her as if just realizing what her presence there meant. "Ah, yes, the Ion!" he said. "It worked! Never thought we'd get you back!" He handed her the candy bar. "This will help you settle in a bit more."

She took the candy bar but raised an eyebrow at him. "Maybe we should discuss things before I... settle in. I wasn't planning to ever see this place again. Or you."

"Ah, of course," said the frog. "I assume you brought the Ion?"

She didn't answer, just waited for him to continue.

He shuffled his large webbed feet and looked from her to the floor and back. "Well, we need the Ion... well, it's a difficult situation, you see..."

"Oh, hell, I'll look for myself." Zephyr got to her feet and walked up to the closest tree trunk, placed her palms against it and dipped her face into the bark, which moved around against her skin like tectonic plates. The tree opened itself up and what she saw inside was reminiscent of a 1920's speakeasy. The doorman, a burly fellow with a pair of intelligent and deadly eyes, seemed to be expecting her and motioned her inside, looking to see she wasn't followed.

"You brought it?" he asked.

She opened her hand and showed him the tiny, green glass tube—the Ion.

He moved out of her way and she walked past tables of drinkers, gawkers, and squawkers, most hardly raising an eye to her use of leather straps as clothing, and made her way to the bar. The bartender, dressed in a top hat and cape, and wearing a villain's mustache, looked her up and down, then mouthed the words, "Ouch."

"The frog?" he asked.

"Who else?"

He shrugged. "Well, what would you like, Zeph? On the house."

"Forty-four magnum. Silver plated." She turned and watched a Scotsman beating on a taiko drum and singing in some other language on the stage. All the walls of the bar were covered in red curtains, and the people at the tables closest to the Scotsman were transfixed on him.

The bartender laughed and slid a martini glass across the bar to her, full of a clear liquid with an olive swirling around at the bottom.

She peered at the drink. "You didn't stiff me…"

He nodded to the glass. "That there's the real deal. Even so, it's on the house."

She looked him in the eye. "I'll pay."

His face turned deadly serious. "I don't do stiffs. Thought you'd know me well enough by now."

She smirked at him and batted her eyes jokingly. "Always so defensive." She reached over to touch his hand but he pulled away before she could.

His head tilted down, the brim of his top hat casting a shadow over his eyes. Then he nodded behind her towards the stage. "You should watch this guy. Everyone comes to see him."

"The Scotsman?" she asked, sort of hoping he wasn't really mad at her. "You like him?"

He shook his head and she turned. The Scotsman was gone and another man was sauntering onto the stage. The man was tall and lanky with the look of someone who hadn't yet come to terms with the fact that his house had burned down that afternoon. He carried a window, a step stool, and a hammer, with a saxophone strapped to his back. Walking to one side of the stage, he set up the step stool and climbed it, hammering the window into place against the red curtain. He climbed down and folded the step stool up, setting it and the hammer off to the side.

The lights dimmed as he somberly approached the microphone, with one spotlight on him and another on the window. The room quieted and everyone turned to him. He looked out at the audience like he was surveying the land of the dead, and made as if to speak—then, thinking better of it, he turned away from them and slung the saxophone around to rest on his hip.

The window slid open and first there was only darkness there behind the opening, then a woman appeared—her hair was the glittering morning sea lapping at her shoulders as if they were the shore, her skin the white sand and her eyes made of driftwood. She looked down between the audience and the stage—completely unaware of anyone else's existence.

The man looked up at her and spoke into the microphone. "I... there's nothing left." His voice vibrated deep like the plucked string of a stand-up bass. "All I have left to give you are the words to this song."

He waited a moment, searching her face for any recognition of his existence—but she continued gazing downward with melancholy eyes, hair stirring gently in a summer's wind. The man swung the saxophone up to his lips, pumping his twisted and squeezed heart through the instrument, transforming it into a piercing banshee's scream. The audience shuddered as his fingers traveled in a slow cat walk over the instrument's golden keys, his face a carved mask of one who is almost too tired to be tortured anymore. His body arched backwards as he belted out wail after unending wail, each note reaching up to the ceiling, circling above the audience like looming vultures—things forced to feed on the dead by the will of gods they'd never prayed to, gods who'd long since disowned them and bestowed upon them such insatiable hunger for the suffering of others.

The banshees of sound descended upon the audience, reaching into hearts and clawing at innards. Zephyr looked at the woman in the window, and as a single tear slid down the woman's cheek, she felt the same tear running down her own, and realized that the woman looked exactly like her. *What if I'm that woman?* she thought to herself, and as soon as the thought passed behind her eyes, Zephyr herself was standing and gazing out of the window, down at an empty section of the stage. A second tear made its way down the valley of her face, and she could smell the salt of the sea thick in the air. She looked over at the man below her, a man in such beautiful agony, and tried to tell him that it was OK, that she loved him and missed him—but no noise passed through her lips, and his eyes were closed as he siphoned the cacophony of sorrow from himself, pouring it up into the air. She looked out over the audience and they were all crying, staring at him lovingly, and she realized each one of them thought they were the woman in the window.

"You're not me!" she tried to yell out. "He's playing for me! These words are mine, he's given them to me."

Then her eye caught her own eye sitting across the room at the bar, the bartender in his top hat behind her, also transfixed on the stage. There were tears running down her face and straps hugging her body. Was her hair blue? She couldn't tell from such a distance in the near-dark.

And then the wailing was gone, the banshees sucked back into the saxophone, leaving the room empty and red in its sudden brightness. Zephyr sat at the bar, eyes still fixed on the empty stage. The window, step stool, and the man were gone.

Zephyr tried to imagine or remember what she saw, tried to bring back the feelings, the love and the loss, the fullness and hollowness, but no memory, image or sound she could conjure up would bring with it the feeling she sought. It was like licking the inside of a wine glass to feel that perfect drunk from the night before.

"Why'd I come here?" she whispered. "Why'd I come back?"

"The frog," said the bartender.

Pressing a hand to her chest, she felt the large metal disc buried deep beneath her skin, felt its magnetic needle spinning so wildly that her flesh was shaking, yearning to burst from the leather straps and vanish into the rest of existence.

"Compass giving you problems?"

She shook her head. "You have a Compass, too. You know, the one you got before you fucking quit. How do you handle existing all the time?"

He motioned behind him, to the rows of bottles. "I keep it drugged."

Her bottom lip quivered. "I want you to unbuckle me."

"That's not in my job description. I'll get canned."

She set the small glass Ion on the bar and swirled her martini glass around in her hand, watching the olive spin about in the clear liquid of the silver plated forty-four magnum. Reaching up, she pushed a strand of blue glittering hair out of her face and behind her ear, then raised the glass and pulled back the hammer with her thumb until it clicked. The bartender raised his hands and tilted his head down, the shadows creeping back over his eyes.

Zephyr was not smiling. "Maybe you'd consider a new line of work."

Travels

Sometimes I travel to the end of my life
and stand at the edge of the world—
leaning on my cane and gazing out.

By then you've already passed away,
left me alone,
but I can feel you around me
like thousands of tiny humming lights,
keeping me warm.

Other times
I like to travel to those last three weeks
we have together—
when we tell each other of stories past,
making each other laugh,
and your smile is so wrinkled,
silly,
and perfect.

*   *   *

Now and then I'll wander
to a few years before that,
to one of the countless summers
we spend at the lake—
the setting sun disappearing
behind treetops
while we sip wine in silence.

Do you want to know one thing I really love to do?
I go back to the first time we sit on that deck,

watching the sunset,
then I look down at both our hands,
wrapped up in each other like lovers,
and I go to the next summer,
and the next, and the next,
watching your hand
grow old
in mine,
becoming ever more beautiful
with all of its
spots and wrinkles.

And it looks as if your hand
is pulling mine through time,
through age—
my hand growing leathery,
calloused,
and dry inside yours.

I go back and forth,
young to old, old to young,
and it's like age itself is breathing
through our hands.

*   *   *

Something else I do—
I sift through the times
we make love.
Like a deck of cards,
there are so many to choose from—

Like when we're old and sagging,
so frail and prone
to bruises and cramps,
and frankly have no business being attracted to one another.
But we are—
we laugh and roll around like teenagers in a fucking barn,
not two old farts on a memory foam mattress
our doctors recommended.

Or decades before,
when we make love *slow*—

gazing into the universe
reflected just behind each others' eyes.
The rhythms of our movements
become the breathing of the earth.
Our moans like small hatchlings,
growing quick and loud
until they become full-grown screams.

And sometimes I like to make love to you for the first time,
as shy and uncertain
as two lovers can be,
trying to please
but trying not to push too far too fast.
We are so fucking awkward that first time, aren't we?
But we are smiling,
and your smile is what does it—
pierces my heart like a harpoon and reels me in.
You pull me up from the ocean and onto the bed,
all wounded,
bleeding,
and blissed out.

From then on,
I am yours.

*   *   *

And sometimes I like to just flirt with you
before anything even happens between us.
When all I know of you is your name,
my desire for you,
and the fear of letting my intensity
scare you away.

But that could never happen—
not with you.

Then at times I travel to just before that,
letting myself keep the knowledge that I'm going to meet you,
while stripping my memory of
who you are—
so that any person I talk to,
anyone I pass on the street,

might be you.

I revel in the joy and excitement
this brings to me.

And once,
every so often,
I travel even earlier—
to a time when your existence isn't even
a glimmer in my world.

Yet I sit, hunched over a desk,
pen in hand,
writing you a love poem
about the life we have together—
before we've even met.

the girl who was the wind

The steering wheel vibrated softly against his forehead, dark blues and violets dancing across his eyelids to the steady beat of Congo drums.

Matt opened his eyes when the song was done—only the hum of the car remained. He turned off the car, got out, and stretched. Gray spirals of stringy cloud floated in the night sky, and the moon was a thumbnail of shining silver. "Tonight it's going to happen," he whispered, breathing in the crisp Autumn air as he crossed the small parking lot. He walked down the winding cobblestone sidewalk, through the twisting sea of sparsely populated shops and restaurants, and into the coffee shop called *The Cove*. The building's ceiling was all exposed beams and planks, and its floor was covered with vintage tables, chairs, and couches, and lit through lampshades so thick that the large room was left dim and cozy.

He pretended to look above the people in front of him in line, at the menu hanging from the ceiling by chains, while actually watching the girl making drinks behind the clunky espresso machine. It had been months now since he'd first seen her and started frequenting The Cove. He'd have to resign himself to being a stalker soon if he didn't talk to her. Her hair was short, black, and sticking up all crazy like ungroomed raven feathers. She was petite and wearing an emerald-green dress.

The extra-pierced and tattooed blond girl was working too, taking peoples' orders. Matt got to the front of the line and the blond girl wasn't there—the two girls had switched. He found himself looking into eyes the color of wet leaves after a rainstorm.

His crush smiled at him. "Hey," she said.

She must have been the prettiest girl he'd ever seen. He wiped the palm of his right hand on his jeans, getting the sweat off in case she offered to shake. "I see you here all the time," said Matt, "and I don't know your name. My name's Matt."

"I know," she said. She leaned forward on the counter and whispered, "My life doesn't go in the same order that yours does."

The music coming through the speakers sounded like the crooning of whales or dolphins, or like music slowed down and played backwards. Matt saw a sadness in her eyes, subtle yet unmoving. It was always there, and he wanted to hold it.

"Will you tell me your name?" he asked.

"You don't remember?"

"You've never told me."

"No, I haven't. I'm called Em." She gave a sideways look to her coworker, then turned back to him. "I'm going on break. I'll bring your drink out to you."

Matt took a seat at a table on the raised area that was used for a stage some nights. Things were going weird, but weird was better than bad.

She came out with two mugs and sat down.

He looked at the mug. "I just realized I didn't tell you what I wanted."

"It's what you usually get."

"I always get something different."

She nodded and sipped from her own mug. "You've never had this before."

The mug was hot against the inside of his hand. "Thank you." It tasted of cream and cinnamon, and of coffee and clove. "What else do you do, Em, besides work here?"

When she looked across the table at him, she wasn't smiling. "I'm going to tell you all of my secrets. That's why you've come here."

Matt leaned forward and let the steam of the coffee waft over his face. His stomach was flipping around inside of him, like one of those underwater ballerinas. "Em... I think it might be best if we saw other people." The green in her eyes didn't so much as shift. He felt like the steam coming from the cup—hardly there at all, and threatening to pass out of existence at any moment.

"I told you that things would be out of place and rearranged," she said, "back when we started this, remember?"

Matt just sipped from his mug.

"It's alright if you don't. I also told you that I'd let you know all my secrets. It's time now, because things are starting not to matter anymore, losing their coherency. I know you can feel it too."

Matt reached out and touched her hand. "Which way are we going now?"

Em shook her head and smiled. "It doesn't matter, Matt. Don't you see that?" She got up, circled the table and knelt down behind him, pressing the side of her face against his ear. When she spoke, her breath passed over the surface of his cheek. "My secret is this: I was the wind. Every time I sleep I still dream about it. There were wings all over my body that would carry me everywhere. Twirling and spinning. I've been not-wind for a year now, and I think I'm losing my ability to keep things in one piece."

"You're turning into wind again?" he asked.

One of her hands crawled like a beetle down his shoulder and over his chest. "Nothing lasts." She reached up and turned his face towards her. Her skin roared with life before his eyes, and the whites of her eyes burned with light around the green orbs inside of them. "I want you to take my virginity," she said, and when their mouths touched it became their hearts touching, breast against breast. He reached towards her face, two fingers dipping into one of her eyes, and his fingers were dripping with searing white light when he pulled them out, and they painted light onto her vibrant skin as he touched her face. He kissed her again, her hands moving through his hair, and he reached far into her with his searching lips—her steaming, pulsing, blue virginity was in his open mouth when he pulled away.

Em wrapped her slender arms around him, sweat and tears running down and mixing with the light smeared on her face. She covered his mouth with an open hand and her blue virginity melted in his mouth, made its way down his throat and to his chest where it started beating like a second heart.

"What was I?" he asked. "What was I before you? Before this?"

"Anything," she said. "Anything at all."

"Have I always been here, in this place?"

Matt looked around and the people in The Cove had become streaks across space, frozen in movement. He was looking down on them, near the ceiling. Em and Matt were no longer sitting, or standing, or lying down. He was floating with her curled up against his chest, her legs wrapped in his, the shifting gravity pulling his hair this way and that. She ran a slender hand along the stitches that went up from his lower belly to his chest. But they weren't stitches—they were shoelaces criss-crossing up the center of him, tied into rabbit-ears near the top.

"Can I *stay* as anything?" he asked.

She kissed his chest and wrapped her hands around his hip bones, squeezing them.

"Em, it's been so long," he said. "I want you to undo me."

She kissed his chest again. "All of this?"

Matt closed his eyes, feeling her warmth against him. "Nothing is meant to last."

He felt her place a strip of cloth over his eyes and tie it behind his head. Her lips passed over his, her breath billowing with scents of clove and coffee, of cinnamon and cream. He was floating there, alone in the darkness. Then he saw a tiny diamond of light suspended there in front of him, a hole in the dark. It widened, and several more diamonds of light appeared, all in a vertical row. He reached out, grabbing the leather-like fabric of the bag he was in and gently parted the openings wider, loosening the strings that held it closed.

He peered out and saw a flurry of wings, each one pulling gently at the edges of leather, prying open the diamonds of space. When there was enough room to get through, he emerged into the thrashing gale, surrounded by feathers—he was spinning and twirling and unfolding, and he stretched out into the wind and the light.

Ghost & The Ballroom

Amidst the crowded ballroom
vexed with vixens,
stained with satin
with dancers flowing steadily from the tap,
I see her.

Unearthly charm,
uneasy whimsy.

"Who are you, ghostly specter?
Whilst mine eyes
they tear,
whilst my heart it bends?"

Yea,
she speaks:

*"I am Inevitable Poetry. Wrapped up tight in half-used candles and
yesterday's whiskey. I'll tear all these gowns off in my mind's eye, let the
caskets prop themselves up against the sky, and hold them ransom for
reasons as of yet unknown."*

My mind it twists like lemon,
cracks like ice dipped in water,
her radiance reaches out to touch
my eyes,
spinning my irises like dual
combination locks.

"Phantom!" I say.
"What do I call thee?

The one with whom madness
doth court ecstasy?"

"*I am Inedible Alchemy. Worrisome and weary, but do you value me? A splintered touch, a movement rushed, like a compass drawing out its radius. Once famous, now left with eyelashes wet with ink, so waking comes with pillows doused in script, carnal secrets written from edge to edge.*"

At the echo of her step
the dancers shed their cloth confines,
falling upon each other
with mouth & skin.
A sea of ecstasy & movement
yet she walks among them,
a silent siren,
a priest on holy land.

"Take my coat with its tales,
take my shoes with their polish,
rip the brim from my top hat
that you may bind me with it!
But do, I pray!
Do tell me your name!
Who affects the world so?"

"*I, sir? I am Insoluble Brevity. I may be quiet, but my words scream for me. The volume is hot in here, so pardon me, while I loosen up my frailty and drink your anonymity.*

"*You can call me Inaudible Ecstasy. Lovers steal away to every crevice of this hall, scraping at the walls, and on their escaping moans I do ride. I do not hide, nor do I lie. Like a word transfixed, I hang in glittering pieces like a chandelier from the rafters. One need only look up. There are those who covet my laughter, to keep in small cages and nurture to adulthood.*

"*But who, pray tell, are you?*

"*And what are you doing in my dream?*"

Two Pieces of Eight

I was peering through layers of neon light (which splashed around like children playing in one of those phony plastic pools) when she interrupted me.

"Care for a dose?" she said.

She was standing beside me and my bar stool, dressed in a full-bodied mechanics uniform. The name tag said, *Mel*. She held a tray with an array of miniature baby bottles, each filled with black liquid.

"I'm not into that sort of thing, Mel," I said.

"Mel's not my real name."

"I did not mean to imply that it was. I was just being polite."

Her hair was long, red, and very curly. She was not incredibly attractive, but she had a button nose. Not that button noses have ever had a particular impression on me, whether positive or negative.

"What are you doing there?" she asked. Her voice had a slight accent, one of those small-town-accents, and I may have been able to place it if I'd ever paid attention to such things.

"Where are you from?" I asked her.

She told me and I let what she said roll right out of my head. Then I said, "I thought this was a strip club. Not that it matters."

"You haven't answered my question," she said.

She seemed short, but I wasn't sure how high my bar stool was. Maybe she was tall.

"Which question?" I asked.

"The only one you haven't answered."

"I'm... how shall I say it? I'm de-rusting quarters."

I turned to the bar in front of me where I had a row of five pint glasses, each filled with a unique, clear concoction which I am under contract not to name, and a shiny quarter standing on edge at the bottom of each glass. Floating atop the liquid in each glass was a thin layer of dark brown flakes of rust.

"Actually, they've been in there much too long," I said.

"Sorry to distract you."

I ignored her, since I've never much liked people who apologize when it is not needed, and I picked up the thin metal spatula that I had lying on a towel. I scooped the layer of rust off the top of each glass and tapped all the dark flakes onto a napkin, making a small black mound. Then I took my tongs and plucked out each quarter in turn, shaking the drops off and then placing them into the left pocket of my long coat. Then with my hand, I pulled out five dirty, rust-encrusted quarters out of my right pocket and plopped one into each glass.

"Why do you feel the need to do that?" asked the girl who was not Mel.

I'd honestly forgotten that she was there. "I thought this was a strip club," I said, trying to change the subject. "Not that it matters."

"You keep saying that. Are you sure it doesn't matter?"

I took a moment to peer around the neon-lit bar. "There are women on stages dancing around poles. They're all wearing many layers of clothing, and all look rather plain. What's this place referred to as?"

"What's with you and names?"

"Maybe I like names. Categories. Organization."

"Do you?"

I shrugged. "Not really."

"Should I leave you alone?"

"No. But maybe."

"You don't like people, do you?"

"I don't. But I'm also afraid of being alone."

I couldn't believe I'd just said such a thing. Never do I give away such measures of my life, and certainly not to strangers, which includes everyone. I wished to collect my quarters and leave, but the coins were in the midst of their de-rustification and I couldn't bring myself to disturb them. *I could just leave,* I thought. *Cut my losses and go.* My body heard these thoughts and wrapped its feet around the legs of the bar stool—because this was not about me, it never was, and my body knew that more than anyone else. My body was never one to stray from a path it had started upon. Stupid and noble, like a dog. I never liked dogs much, but I don't mind my body most of the time.

She touched my shoulder. The back of her hand was smeared with grease and oil.

"I could fix you," she said.

"What?"

Her thighs pressed up against my leg and the heavy pocket full of quarters swung to and fro below us like the pendulum of so many grandfather clocks. "I said I could... *fix*... you." And when she said the word *fix* her teeth scraped so slowly over her bottom lip that I had no choice but to imagine those white soldiers of bone raking across my own jaw, my chin, my cheekbones. I wobbled in my seat as my chest began to lose its footing underneath my shirt.

"I can do that," she added, setting the tray of bottles on the bar.

"I—I thought—thought this was a strip club," I said. *Shit-shit-shit! Why'd I come here? What is this place?* The quarters and the pint glasses swam around in the corner of my vision. I was getting light-headed and losing circulation in my feet which were latched on to the rungs of the bar stool, anchoring me with such passion to a completely unanchored object.

Then her hand was on my forehead, like a mother checking a child for a fever.

"Don't do that," I said. "You mustn't."

Her mouth opened wide like a snake's, and my forehead unhinged to swing open underneath her hand, leaving my head's inner parts naked and unprotected. From the darkness between her lips emerged a gleaming metal arm which was actually more like an oversized wrench with an elbow, slick with dripping saliva as it reached up to that unknown territory above my eyes.

Then my hands were on her face, trying to push her from me, my bar stool rocking beneath me up onto two legs, my feet still anchoring me to it. I pulled my head away from the metallic extension, dodging this way and that as sticky saliva and grease drooled onto my face. Realizing that my fate and the fate of the operation were fused with the events of the next several seconds, I reached through the cloud of morality and conscience that I keep as a wall around my person and grabbed at her chest, half-blinded I was by the excessive amounts of saliva running through my eyes. I had closed the small gap between us by doing this, and the wrench-hand slipped into the opening in my forehead, gripping on tight to the things inside, but not before I grabbed the name tag on her uniform and ripped it off.

She began choking and coughing, each spasm traveling across the metal arm and severely loosening the things in the top-most section of my head. I struggled to pull the cursed thing out of me, but every moment found me weaker than the last. My feet unhooked from the bar stool and in a last-ditch effort I and my body teamed up, putting a foot on her chest and shoving with every drop of strength we had left. I pulled free of her and she slouched sideways onto the bar, and the end of the wrench-arm was holding a fist-sized motor with broken wires dangling from it. Before my eyes the motor began to darken with rust—layer after layer it corroded until it was completely unrecognizable. The brown decay spread like liquid over the wrench-hand and down the length of the arm. I did not see what became of the girl who was not Mel, for I had lost feeling throughout most of my body and was tipping backwards in my bar stool, and as I fell I felt my body let go of such ideas as solidity, force, and consumption. It had to do this, of course, sacrificing itself so that the whole of the job was not lost, so that not all of my efforts were in vain. I would have done the same thing if I were in its shoes.

It is a strange feeling to have your body break up into so many small, near-identical coins—to go from being one to being thousands in a mere second. Before I hit the ground, it was done. The transformation was complete. It was not supposed to end this way, but I could no longer care. For, when I hit the ground as many, the sound that arose was so profoundly pleasant to me that I at once released from inside myself all other lingering emotions. I cannot say if I would have found the sound so pleasing if somebody *else* had fallen to the ground as thousands of quarters, and the feeling arising inside of me was not unlike being deep in the forest and hearing thousands of crickets erupt into chorus. Perhaps I felt this way because I was hearing myself as something new, something fresh. But the one thing that rang out through my consciousness, soft as a whisper and as unobtrusive as a speck of dust dancing in the barely-stirring air, was: *Now I am multiple, now I am not alone, and I shall never be alone again.*

The Study

He sets his book down upon his lap and squeezes his temples, but no amount of concentration on his part will quench the hollow whispers. Looking up, across the study he sees the lady lying in the wall as if it were a shallow pond, a cloak pulled tight over her body with thin, skeletal hands. She stares at the ground with her dark, lightless eyes, but he feels her watching him from the periphery, as she waits there between the two dusty bookshelves like an ancestral sword hanging upon the wall.

Setting his book on the armrest of the reading chair, he stands and walks to her, taking her into his arms as if to kiss her. But as she croons her head back to meet his lips, he kneels down before her and pulls open her cloak—and there, instead of her belly, is a second face, ghostly in pallor and solidity—and it is this face which he kisses instead.

Her hands reach down, her fingers wrapping and entwining into his tangle of hair. He closes his eyes and gives himself completely to this ghost face as it reaches into his mind with an invisible tongue, finds the switches to his memories, and flips them off in quick succession.

Age of the Moth

The small wooden room is left pale by a thick layer of dust covering the bookshelves, floors, and walls. Cobwebs hang like orbs of static up in the corners of the room, the flickering candlelight giving them the illusion of swaying and dancing.

At the desk, Elias hunches forward with a bulky see-close device he'd constructed from remnants of telescopes strapped over his eyes. With a tiny pair of tweezers, he ever-so-gently pulls at the moth's leg, stretching it out. Then he moves it back, carefully watching each joint.

The moth is held suspended in a contraption not unlike a picture frame, with tiny metal clamps on wires leading from the frame to the edges of the moth's wings and body. Only one half of the moth's body has legs, and it still lacks antennae.

Shadows flicker across Elias' vision and he spins around, startled. But all he sees are blurry colors swimming around before him. He struggles to pull the see-close off his head without pulling off his spectacles.

"I'm sorry," says Simeryn. His daughter stands there in a white nightgown, her hair long and blonde. "I couldn't sleep."

Elias sets the see-close on the desk, making sure to keep himself between the moth and his daughter. "I don't blame you," he says. "These are strange times. You don't see me sleeping." He gets to his feet, walks over and puts his hands on her shoulders.

"I keep thinking we should go back," she says.

Elias has become so poor at remembering things—her age flutters before his eyes like an uncatchable insect. She can't be any older than thirteen, yet must be older than sixteen. "There is no back, my dear," he tells her. "There's nothing behind us."

She nods and looks down.

"But I've got a secret," he says. "I'm making something for you. I'll be finished with it soon." Simeryn looks up towards the desk and he moves to block her gaze. "But you can't see it yet."

"Maybe if I read I'll be able to sleep," says his daughter.

"Ah." Elias walks over to a bookshelf and runs a finger along the spines of the dusty books. "I've got one I think you'll enjoy." He pulls out the book, turns, and hands it to her. She looks down at the title etched into the heavy book's cover—*The Properties of Disintegration*. "It's a fairytale, of sorts."

She nods. "This'll do," she says, and when Elias looks up at her she is standing farther away, in the center of a hole ripped out of the air. Behind her, rather than the dusty wooden walls, there is the wet brick wall of an alley. Overturned trash cans and paper litter the ground around her. Her hair is pulled back into a ponytail, and she's wearing a jean jacket, boots, and a skirt.

Now Elias is looking down on her from high above, looking out of a small, dirty window, down into the alley as she strides away from him across the shallow black puddles.

He turns away from the window, back to the bathroom mirror, his face half-covered with shaving cream, and continues shaving around his black mustache and goatee. Several gray hairs are interspersed with the black, and his skin is worn and creased like an old, reliable coat. He throws water onto his face and dries it off with a towel, then reaches into his breast pocket and pulls out a small mechanical moth. The little creature clicks and squeaks in the palm of his hand as it stretches out with its opaque wings. Elias takes his shaving razor and slices open the tip of his finger, and the moth walks up to the cut, unrolls its metal proboscis and sticks the end into the torn flesh. He can hear the gears inside of it turning and oiling themselves. Its transparent wings begin filling with patterns of red, orange, and brown—slowly, like two identical galaxies bursting into existence.

The moth backs away from the cut, turns and looks out the dirty window.

Elias glances at himself in the mirror and his hair is now all gray, his cheeks sunken like two shallow craters. "Wait," he whispers to the moth.

The insect turns to him, flicking its silvery antennae about in the air, its insides clicking and whirring.

"I've got nothing left," Elias whispers. "Just shades of colors no one remembers. Why would anyone want that?"

The moth walks down his finger to his palm, then to the edge of his hand and motions down towards the razor sitting on the sink. Some of the blood from Elias' finger sits drying on the blade.

Suddenly Elias feels thousands of tiny, invisible threads tied to every part of his body, each of them leading in a different direction. Some go out the window, some to the ceiling and walls and the mirror. And against the wall next to the mirror the threads weave together with other threads, creating patterns and designs that somehow recreate his whole life up to that point, capturing the essence of each event and moment in a series of symbols—all in an insignificantly small section of the wall about the size of his fist. Like a gear in a machine, he has turned and continues to turn, ending up in the same places over and over again, the same happiness and depression unending.

He sets his hand upon his own shoulder and the moth climbs down, then he picks up the razor. For a moment he considers cutting the strings, but he'd still be the same gear in the same machine—just in-operational. So instead he presses the blade against his wrist and pushes it down. As he drags it across the skin he can see all the tiny strings begin to snap one at a time, flicking about madly like worms cut in half on the sidewalk.

Elias' skin hardens and thickens until he is left completely frozen, standing there like a statue with the blade lodged into his wrist. His skin quickly pales and turns gray. His eyes too, behind his spectacles, cloud over with a thickening white layer. He stands immobile as the last few strings snap and writhe around in the air blindly before twitching and falling limply onto the floor with the rest of their brethren.

When the last string snaps, Elias feels gravity shift as his body tips and falls sideways onto the tiled floor. All he sees is the cloudy white that covers his eyes—and he feels only numbness. He waits, but soon grows restless and begins to turn and twist about inside the wall of hardened, gray skin. The flesh feels uncomfortable, and sudden claustrophobia grips him. He writhes around inside of the walls, spinning and pushing against them in vain. Finally, he finds a weak spot and beats against it, hearing it crack as it slowly comes apart. He positions himself so that he can push against another wall, pressing against the weak spot. Pain rages through him as he forces the cracked wall open and breaks through into the cold, wet air. He crawls away from the suffocating gray walls, his large metallic legs clicking and his body whirring as he walks. He turns to see the shell that was Elias there on the bathroom floor, all gray and cracked with the razor still shoved into its wrist.

He stretches his thorax, stretches his wings out towards the walls and ceiling. Then he turns towards a hole torn out of space, through which he sees Simeryn dancing in a nightclub amidst a hundred others—blue and green lights pulsing in chaotic beams to the booming of music. Now he's looking down on her from high up in the rafters, crawling along wooden rafters like a spider.

The moth lets go of the rafters and flitters downward, neon lights and pulsing noise swirling in a cacophony of echoes and reflections. The metal insect weaves over and around the dancers, through musty clouds of perfume and human stench, to land on the shoulder of Simeryn's jean jacket. He grips onto the jacket with hooked metal legs as she sways and turns to the primordial pounding.

Her eyes are rimmed with silver and her lips are dark blue. He sees a thousand versions of her at once reflected in his many eyes.

The rest of her tribe are made up in different fashions, invoking so many gods as they move and chant inside the colorful, pulsing darkness. The moth crawls closer to her face and hums mechanical lullabies into her ear, and instantly the lullabies begin to crawl down into her eardrum and change her. He can hear her organs and juices drying up, her organs sucking up all the moisture around them as they start converting into metals—her heart begins pumping copper, her lungs start to produce gold dust, and her womb begins to coat its walls with shiny brass. Her movements become more repetitive and sharp—a determination beginning to wash over her.

Then, before the moth is finished with the lullaby, she reaches up and grabs the moth in her hand. It struggles but is already weakened from weaving its tune into her. She is moving, walking, but the moth is enclosed and cannot tell where she is taking it.

When she finally lets it go, the moth finds itself on a table. It has just enough time to see the hammer coming towards it before the metal tool slams down onto its machine body, ripping through it like a wrecking ball, decimating its mechanical self without a shred of doubt.

Then there is no movement—the moth's body clicks and makes noise but is no longer capable of moving. It sees the wooden room behind her with its many eyes, the bookshelf layered in dust, the see-close device sitting on the desk nearby. She can't be any older than thirty, but her hair is long and gray. Her shirt is off, and underneath her bra, over her stomach, a little blonde girl is tattooing a picture—a large depiction of a shattered insectile machine. The little girl looks back at the moth as she draws—both her eyes and the older lady's are cold and undistracted.

The moth's body stops whirring and clicking, and he can feel his form slipping between his fingers like quickly melting ice. The old lady and the girl drift off like clouds. He feels his memories and natures become transparent, and a sort of levity takes hold of him and he sighs. "Ah..." All thought fades, his sins fall off like ash and he is pulled away, cut from the world like a piece of thread. "This is the part where I get to go home again, isn't it?"

The Gambler's Fate

She comes to me
crawling out of the blue
her body a mass of shadows and algae

I want only to gaze on her
but my body won't stop struggling
struggling for air it cannot have

I yearn to be free
to take her up to my world with me
but my feet and legs
encased in so much rock and chain

The last bubbles slip from between my teeth
and she presses two fingers to my lips

Deep eyes calm me

My lungs erupt somewhere like twin volcanoes
silently
lighting up the world before me
with tiny bursts of orange and red

She picks my memories like flower petals
letting each one float off with the current
like so many lonely dancers

Until there is only one memory left
and this world becomes all I've known
this blue world
this body of mine with its legs of stone

Her with hair like a wild halo
skin reflective and smooth
as she rests her head against me

I am half statue and half myth
half heart and half jewel
half galaxy and half form

With her there in the dark and the blue
my first and last lover

and me with hands empty of dice
empty of playing cards
empty of lies
holding nothing but her
and the growing quiet

Dame of the Eagle Saloon

Yeah, I loved you
eyeing me from across the room
fingers walkin' down that
talkin' trumpet
your eyes & mine
having just met
the first time

Of course I'd seen your kind
all new & exploring
you could not be
more green

Yeah, I knew you'd
saunter up to my table
& bite on my feigned surprise
Was it my hair that you complimented?
Or was it my lace, my dress,
my countenance?

Spillin' words & splashin' gin
my mind soaked & slippin'
headlong towards
what I knew was wrong
Oh, but there you were
touching me with the fingertips
of your eyes
pacifying the cries
of my thoughts
your words hooking into
sucking at my wants

I knew I'd fall into
your fistful of sheets
that your fingers would meet
pressing down on the keys
of my spine
lion & sheep
which am I?

Yeah, I loved you
my name pouring from your lips
my mane purring against your hips
my skin
your skin
drips

Face against hot face
rolling bodies of steam
I, an unhinged dream
but what are you to me?

Yeah, I loved you
but my past is laced with poisons
dark & dazed liaisons
crumpled against the wall
and bubbling
against reason

Yet each night I met with you
your moans pulling me
into a world where
my nightmares
held no truth

Oh and how you'd gaze down at me
skin bursting with that
brazen heat
the moonlit curtains
giving you glowing wings
"Baby, you should not be with me."

Oh how I'd pull you on top of me
only you could topple me
but you couldn't stop the things

that I had come to be

Yeah, I warned you
of the figures keeping warm
in my shadow
yet you had to know
had to press for more
until I could not keep you
protected
undetected
"Baby, they will shred you."

Yeah, I let you
distill in me
pretty stills & imagery
each caress each pretty word
buzzing across my skin
pollinating
killing off my questions

If only I could
live between your sheets
where the two of our lives meet
where I am you
you are me

But here we are
in the middle of the empty street
while everybody else dreams
I told you
they'd never stop looking for me

Yeah, I loved you
the stars above begin to cry
I lift up my dress
reaching down between my thighs
a small revolver
gleaming silver in streetlight

Yeah, I loved you
but I will not let them take you

goodbye

Snake Kingdom

The first thing Max remembers is falling sideways onto the floor of the apartment, with the shag carpet soft against his head and shoulder. The ropes tying his arms, legs and bare chest to a wooden chair are not so soft, and his flesh burns where the ropes touch him. His head sags—a dazed and crooked arrow pointing towards the floor.

This is nonsense, he thinks to himself. I'd never live somewhere with shag carpet.

An old television sitting directly in front of him turns on and, as the tubes warm up, shows a green and golden snake skimming over the surface of water in a swamp. "Snake Kingdom will return after these messages," an announcer promises.

Then a horrid honky-tonk riff begins bungling its way out of the TV and an overhead shot of a used car lot appears, complete with balloons, multicolored flags, and big numbers painted onto car windows. A man in a cowboy hat with a toothpick in his mouth is standing amidst the sea of cars. He seems to look Max right in the eye.

"I've been selling cars for forty years," the man bellows with a twang. Beads of sweat have formed on his forehead and Max wonders how many times this man's had to say the same lines over and over again. "And all the questions you could possibly ask yourself about getting a pre-owned truck or car—you can take all those and shave 'em down till they look like a newborn baby calf's belly and I'll tell ya what, they all become the same question," the man raises a single finger, "Where do you get your happiness from?"

An explosion of white cascades across the TV screen and a cardboard milk carton lands on its side in front of Max's head. He can't make out the man in the cowboy hat behind the white liquid covering the screen, but the man keeps on saying the same thing, like a skipping record: "Where do you get your happiness from? Where do you get your happiness from?"

There's a comic strip on the side of the milk carton. The comic strip is only three panels long, but somehow conveys the story of two boys: one boy drinks milk and ends up going to college and buying up all four railroads in the city and having a wife and two kids who also drink milk, while the other boy doesn't drink milk and goes to jail for not being able to pay rent after landing on one of the first boy's railroad lines.

The milk carton and the floor are suddenly spinning as Max's chair is pulled back to its rightful position and spun around to face the rest of the room, which consists of a cardboard box that he and three other people are sitting at. There's a deck of cards sitting on top of the box, and each of the other people are sitting on upside-down milk crates. A man as black as midnight sits on Max's left, glaring at him with heavy, golden eyes. "If you cheat again, it's the window," he says.

Max looks down at the chair and the ropes. "Can't rightly cheat in this getup. Now if you could untie my arms, give me a long sleeve shirt and an extra deck, maybe then we could talk."

The lady to Max's right covers her mouth to stifle a giggle. She's Asian and wearing a gold and white kimono.

"He's faking," says the man sitting directly across from Max. The man is bald and muscular and has words tattooed in different fonts and languages all over his torso and arms. He pulls down his circular shades and smirks at Max. "Dude's fucked up," he says to the midnight man. "Don't know day from night. He's just trying not to let on."

The midnight man shakes his head. "He's playing you," he says. "This cheat wants you to think he don't know what's going on." He pulls out a burlap sack and tosses it onto Max's lap. Max lurches backward as the bag begins to writhe around and hiss, and the midnight man reaches out and grabs Max's chair to keep it from tipping over. "Settle down, cheating man," he says, "or she's gonna get jumpy."

The kimono lady giggles again. Her long hair is pulled into a ponytail, her face is ghost white, and her mascara makes her eyes look like they're on fire. She sits with the posture every parent wishes their child had. Max wonders for half a second if she drinks milk, but his attention is pulled back to the writhing sack on his lap.

"Just keep your cool," says the midnight man.

Max laughs and grits his teeth. The sack feels like thick-fingered hands trying to push open his thighs. "Take it away," he says, turning his head to look toward the wall. Only there isn't a wall anymore, but a hallway. The light in the hallway is sharp and violet, and someone is crawling slowly down the hallway towards the four of them—a woman wrapped in some sort of gray cloth. Every time she reaches forward to pull herself further towards them, a burst of television static crackles through the air.

"Who are you?" Max whispers.

He hears the word man as if from another room. "Dude's fucked up."

Then the crawling woman looks up into Max's eyes. Her hair is long, tangled, and dirty, and he knows her from somewhere. Beside him the kimono lady moves—she flitters up through the air as if she's made of paper, towards the woman in the hallway. The gray cloth covering the crawling woman unfurls like a dozen flags up into the air—and he realizes that the cloth is really a pair of enormous, faded gray wings coming from the crawling woman's back, folding out to engulf the entirety of the hallway—which is suddenly enormous.

The kimono lady glides down behind the winged woman like a paper puppet, gripping a handful of the woman's hair and pulling it back so that the woman's bare chest faces the table of would-be card players.

Max struggles against the ropes, but they burn into his flesh and stand their ground. He looks at the two others: "You have to do something!" The burlap sack jumps around violently in his lap.

"Dude's fucked up," echoes the voice of the word man, but the man's lips don't move.

Max turns back towards the violet hallway and the winged woman screams out a mouthful of television static that stains and scratches the air. The kimono lady looks up to the ceiling and closes her eyes in utter ecstasy as a knife appears in her open hand, her white spider-leg fingers wrapping around the hilt.

"*What's she doing?*" cries Max. "Who is that woman? I know her from somewhere!"

The violet walls spiral around the two women as the winged woman grabs the kimono lady's hand with the knife in it. The kimono lady's face contorts with rage as she struggles to pull away, but the winged lady has a fierce grip and pulls the point of the blade between her own bare breasts, the flesh there giving way and swapping blood for metal.

Max screams and lunges towards them, trying with all his will to break his bindings. His chair rocks and tips and the midnight man reaches out but is too late—Max is falling once again towards the shag carpet. Pain scrapes like two needles across his chest and he looks down to see the snake's head dislodge itself from his skin just before his head connects with the floor.

"That hardly bodes well for the future of the game," he hears the word man say.

A drum pounds slow and loud somewhere far away. Max sees mountains and dark fields stretching out under a violent yellow sky. An old man with no eyes and no eyelids sits in a rocking chair on the front porch of a hollow shack, patiently waiting and tapping slowly on the armrest of the chair. His thin, wrinkled fingers *thump... thump... thumping* away.

Thump... calling to Max, beckoning him.

"I am a rat," whispers Max, "and I have a date with the piper."

Thump...

Something touches Max's face and he opens his eyes to find himself on his back, tied to the chair and staring up at the ceiling. Then two eyes are there, green as emeralds, surrounded by flesh the color of tree leaves, with eyelashes and eyebrows of seaweed. At first, he thinks it is the woman with the wings, but this is someone else—someone new. Her face is so close to his, and he can feel her sex in the air between them like mist.

Thump...

"I can help you out of this chair," she whispers, her breath playing across his cheek.

"The old man send you?" he asks.

Thump...

She looks down at his lips. Her own lips glisten in their greenness. "You just have to love me," she says. "Just for a little while."

"What about the woman with the wings?"

Thump...

"You don't *believe* in angels."

He tries to shrug but his body is numb and tingling. "I'll let you believe that I love you. But you're not my kind of poison."

Thump...

A tingling feeling travels slow down the center of his torso and drifts over his loins. "I'll become your kind of poison," she says.

Max closes his eyes. "That would be nice."

Thump...

"You gonna fuckin' cut the deck?" grumbles the voice of the midnight man.

Max feels the girl curl up on top of him like a cat. Maybe he can let himself pretend to love this one for a while.

Thump...

"Dude's fucked up. Don't know day from night."

"The question you have to ask yourself is, 'Where do you get your happiness from?'"

The girl is warm on top of his tingling body, her head resting in the hollow of his neck. "I love you," she whispers. "I'll take care of all your woes."

The kimono lady giggles somewhere far off, and he can smell the angel's blood thick on the Japanese robes wrapped around her.

"I know," he says.

"Max..." she whispers.

"Yes," he says, answering her question before she can ask it.

Dreaming Red

Part I

The air in the living room was thick and musty. The coffee table was a collage of paper plates, empty glasses, and a pizza box. Alex sat on the floor, with his back against his couch and a bottle of Jack Daniels in his hand, his eyes fixed on the one clean spot on his coffee table. If only that spot would grow to consume, alter, and morph the rest of the apartment. If only that spot would spread to him, crawling across his body, simplifying all aspects of himself.

He glanced down at a framed photo lying on the floor. The woman in it smiled back up at him, her red hair reaching out towards him through the glass, like vines climbing in spirals up invisible balcony rails. He looked at the phone on the table, sitting there on its throne of wrappers and ketchup packets, and took a drag of his cigarette. Stretching his jaw, he squeezed the back of his neck with one hand.

Meow.

Dora's mouth opened impossibly wide as she stretched and walked over.

"Hey Dora," he said as he stroked her back. "Does any of it make sense to you?" He smiled and took another drag. "Me neither."

*   *   *

The next morning, Alex walked into the small office of Montigate & Sons Fine Imports, a small little business lost among the antique shops, quaint restaurants, and small Southern mansions in New Orleans' Garden District. Levi was busy at the desk writing down addresses on a torn piece of paper.

"Sorry I'm late," said Alex.

Levi glanced up at the computer screen. "Actually, you're right on time."

"Really? Nevermind then." Alex walked past him to the coffee maker.

"You look like shit, man," said Levi, leaning back in his chair.

Alex ran a hand through his hair and faked a smile. "Well, I *feel* fantastic."

"You've been thinking about Jamie."

Alex poured himself a cup of bad coffee.

Levi shook his head. "You didn't call her, did you?"

"No."

"Good. Every time you get back with her it's worse. You two don't match, man. She's a nice girl, Alex. Just not for you."

Alex shrugged. "I didn't call her. Let's drop it." He sipped his coffee, grimaced and coughed. It was horrible. He poured some hazelnut powdered creamer into the cup and stirred it with a tiny straw, making it horrible in a different way.

"Hey, fine." Levi drank his own coffee. "I've got a friend you should meet."

Alex walked towards the door to the back room. "I'm not interested in meeting anyone, Levi."

"She's a med student. I thought you could talk to her about your sleeping problem."

Alex stopped and turned. "It's not that bad of a problem."

"Maybe in your world, falling unconscious is part of a healthy everyday life, but to most of mankind it's fucking weird and scary."

Alex managed a smile and shrugged. "Not much I can do about it."

"You can talk to my friend. She's smart, and it won't cost anything."

Alex opened the door to the back room.

"Alex?"

"I'll talk to her," he said as he walked in and closed the door.

As he did three days each week, Alex sat at his desk, wrapped fine china, vases, and the like in bubble wrap, placed them in boxes of packing peanuts and taped them shut. He printed out labels, stuck them to the appropriate boxes, and stacked them in piles. Wrap, tape, label, and stack.

In the afternoon Levi walked in and leaned on the door frame, drinking a fresh cup of bad coffee. "Meet me for drinks tonight," he said.

"I don't know." Alex rubbed his eyes.

"Look, man. It's not good for you to be alone all the time. I'm meeting a couple people at Bar Tonique at eight, in the Quarter. You like Bar Tonique. It'll get you out of your neighborhood, and there'll be other people. Really chill. I'll see if my med school friend can come too."

"I'll see."

"Promise me, Alex. I'm serious. I'm worried about you—you're my oldest friend."

"Yeah all right, I'll be there." He looked over at Levi. "I will."

"Good. I'm off to meet a client—that Tom Saco guy." Levi smiled. "Totally loaded. Said he heard about us from that Bardell deal we did a year back."

"Sounds great."

"Lock up when you leave."

Then Alex was alone taping, labeling, and stacking boxes. Wrap, tape, label, and stack. Alex's eyes grew heavy and distant, and then they closed...

When he opened them he was in another room which was dimly lit and empty, sitting on a wooden chair. It looked like his apartment, only without his furniture. There were a few tables scattered about and a big wooden door. He turned in the chair and found himself face-to-face with a young girl.

"Yo, sleepyhead!" she yelled.

Alex jumped back, tumbling off the chair and onto the floor.

The girl was crouched atop a wooden dining table above him. Her bright red hair fell in long, thin braids nearly to her shoulders, and she wore a loose patchwork garment that vaguely resembled a kimono. If he had to guess, he'd place her at about twelve years old.

"Who are you?" he asked.

She squinted one eye and cocked her head. "Ah, I get it!" She climbed like a lizard down onto the chair he'd fallen off. "I am the living labyrinth of lavender that adventurers walk, all of them practically guaranteed certain doom at the hands of my lacerous liavixes." She leapt off the chair, spinning into the air and landing next to him in a crouch, pushing her face up into his. "Now, what are *you*?"

Alex looked down at his hand—it seemed normal. "A dream? Is this what the inside of my head looks like?" He glanced around at the chair and the tables, the blank walls.

"Oh, really now!" she said and galloped quickly across the floor.

His eyes followed her as she disappeared through the door, which became the door to his office, and he was sitting at his desk. Alex stood up slowly, his limbs still numb like he'd been sleeping for hours. He walked to the door and looked into Levi's office, which looked like it always did— no little red-haired girl, no Levi.

He looked at the wall clock. "Shit." He grabbed his jacket and walked out, locking the front door behind him.

*　　　　*　　　　*

Alex smoked a cigarette on the sidewalk of Saint Charles Avenue, watching from a distance as Jaime opened the gate to the converted

Southern mansion that was her apartment building. She walked up the steps and fumbled through her purse for her keys. There were still a couple hours' worth of sunlight left, and a streetcar rattled and squealed its way through the middle of the street, cars whizzing by on either side of it.

"It's the green one," he whispered.

She tried a key to no avail, ruffled through the keys and tried again. He inhaled, trying to soak up anything he could from her, from this non-encounter.

The door opened, and she was gone.

A little blonde girl skipping down the sidewalk stopped in front of him. "You alright?" she asked.

Alex dropped the cigarette and stepped on it. He crossed his arms and shook his head. "I don't know."

"Anything I can do to help?"

Alex smiled. "Naw, you go play. Thanks, though."

She shrugged and went back to skipping down the sidewalk.

Alex walked down the street and into Audubon Park, where he found a bench to people watch. He watched couples walk by, watched the children on the playground in the distance, watched people walking their dogs or playing with them. He looked down at the ants crawling around the tips of his shoes.

When he looked back up, he was sitting at a table in that same dim, mostly-empty room—the one that looked like his apartment. There was a game board in front of him with several chess-like pieces on it. To his left sat the young red-haired girl and across from him was a thin bald man with sunglasses and no shirt. The three of them each held five playing cards.

The red-haired girl burst out laughing.

"Shoulda seen the turtle's face, Red!" said the bald man.

Ah, yes! Alex thought to himself. *Her name is Red.*

Alex's eyes kept stealing over to look at a wooden door across the room which was barricaded with a table and sofa. He just knew something was on the other side—something that really wanted to come through. If this was his apartment, that would be the bathroom.

The bald man caught his gaze, then placed a card down and moved a piece across the board. "Nothing we can do about it now," he muttered. "What's done is done."

Alex twisted his mouth, looked over his hand of cards, and placed one face up on the board. He tipped a short piece onto it's side, then glanced up to see the red-haired girl smile while the bald man glared at him.

"I think that's game," said Alex.

"Sometimes the hardest thing to see is the obvious," the bald man said as he turned the five cards around in his hand and placed them onto the table. He smiled at Alex and moved a piece onto the middle of the board.

"You came into the game too late, young man."

Red put her cards face down on the table. "Good game! And there are always future and past games to look forward to." She leaned over the makeshift table, reached in front of Alex and snapped her fingers—"Alex, wake up."

He backed away from her, annoyed. "What do you mean, 'wake up'?"

"Looks fine to me," said the bald man as he gathered up all the cards in order to shuffle again.

Red grabbed Alex's shoulders and shook him.

"What!" he said, batting her hands away. "Stop that."

Then, instead of the dim room behind the girl, there were branches, trees, and sky. "Alex, wake up!" she said, her voice growing deeper.

"I'm just playing Downs and Spades!" Alex said.

Red's braids unspun themselves and grew longer, and she grew into a woman before him. Suddenly he was looking up at Jamie, who was sitting next to him while he was curled up on a park bench.

"Jamie?" he said, squeezing his eyes. "What are you doing here?"

"This is the park, Alex. I found you passed out on a bench."

Alex looked around. The sun had set, and it was getting dark.

"What's 'down and spades?'" she asked.

Alex shook his head. "What?"

"Are you drunk?"

Alex leaned forward, rubbing his eyes. "No. Just keep falling asleep. Weird dreams, too. So strange."

"What do you mean you *keep falling asleep*?"

Alex shrugged. "Don't know. Probably my diet or something. I just... doze off."

"Have you seen a doctor?"

He ran his fingers through his hair and sat back against the bench. His body was sore from lying on the metal. "No insurance."

"Have you told Levi?"

"Yeah," he laughed. "But he's not a doctor."

Jamie put her hand to her forehead. "Alex, come to my apartment. I'll cook you something healthy. I've got some herbal tea you might like."

Alex looked at her and shook his head. "Jamie, it's not gonna happen."

She laughed. "You never used to mind my cooking."

He got to his feet. "Look, I'm just not going with you."

Jamie leaned forward on the bench. "Fuck you, Alex," she whispered. When she looked up her eyes were wet. "Out of all the parks, you go out of your way to come to this one. All the time, watching me." She got to her feet. "Do you blame me, Alex?"

"No. No, of course not."

"You know, I can't deal with you right now." She turned and walked away from him, through the park and towards her apartment building.

Alex sniffed, then clenched and unclenched his fists. "Damn it."

Part II

Sunlight poured like honey through the green leaves above as Alex walked through the dense shrubbery and oak trees. He stopped when he saw Red, standing there wearing a jean jacket and a skirt.

"Red, why are you here?"

Red smiled at him. "I'm here to find *you*. Where have you been?"

He walked up to her, shaking his head. "I've been right here." He grabbed her and hugged her tightly.

"Come on, Alex," she said, laughing. "It hasn't been that long." She pushed him away, and her hair was now long and blonde. "You always were the silly one." She looked behind him and raised an eyebrow. "What's that?" Alex turned to look and she slapped him on the shoulder. "Now you're it!" she yelled and darted away into the thick shrubbery and trees.

He took off after her, smiling, but the sound of her shoes crunching through the leaves suddenly stopped. He looked around, but couldn't see or hear anything but the wind blowing through the branches above. "Rachel?" he called out. He turned around, peering through the trees. "Rachel!" he yelled. "Rachel, this isn't a game!"

Taking a step forward, Alex found himself in a large, dark-red room. There were pictures and paintings on the walls along with a large brass-framed mirror. Alex turned to see Jamie standing behind him wearing a jean jacket and a skirt, her red hair pulled back into a ponytail.

She smiled as she looked at the walls of the room. "What is this place?"

Alex followed her gaze. "This is my friend's house."

"I like the paintings."

"That's why I wanted you to come here—to show you."

"Did you paint them for me?"

He shook his head and walked towards the mirror. "I don't know who painted them." He reached out towards the mirror but kept his distance.

"Always playing make-believe," she laughed.

He looked back at her and all the paintings were now drawn in crayon on paper, taped to the walls with masking tape. Turning back to the mirror, it had become a large crayon drawing of himself reaching towards it. He dropped his hand and stepped back, but it didn't change.

When he turned back around, instead of Jamie there was a little blonde girl wearing a jean jacket and a skirt. She took his hand, which was now the hand of a little boy, and she slipped a woven bracelet around his wrist. The red walls behind her dripped and melted away, replaced by trees and sunlight.

Alex shook his head. "I can't."

"Come with me, Alex."

"Rachel, you know I can't. Don't do this to me."

He opened his eyes and sat back against his sofa with Dora cuddled up on his lap. He picked up his Jack and Coke and finished it off. He reached into the pile of fast food wrappers and paper bags on his coffee table, pulled out a phone, then dialed.

He licked his lips and took a deep breath. "Jamie, it's Alex. Can you... can you meet me at the park?"

*   *   *

Alex walked through Audubon Park with his hands in his pockets, walking into a cluster of trees and finding the little creek. The only sounds he heard were the whispers of wind and the trickling of water in the creek.

Up ahead, he saw Red walking alongside the creek, and when she saw him she ran out of sight.

"Wait!" yelled Alex and took off after her. He rounded a bend of trees and the little blonde girl was there, crouched down by the creek.

She looked up and smiled, then stood up. "You came here to rescue me!"

Alex's mouth quivered. "I can't..." He shook his head. "I'm sorry..."

"Did you bring a sword? There are dragons everywhere! They're small ones, and camouflage into the bark of the trees. But they'll *gut* you like that," she said, snapping her fingers.

"I... I don't know how."

"You used to know how!" She looked up at him and grabbed his arms, shaking him.

"You don't understand." He knelt in the dirt so that he was eye level with her. "You don't know what you're asking me."

She grabbed his face, placed her thumbs above his eyes and gently pushed his eyelids down over his eyes. "Please. Please remember."

When Alex's eyes closed he was in the empty apartment with Red standing across from him.

Red smiled and pointed to her forehead. "You sure you want what's in here, mister?"

Alex half-laughed, then he shrugged. "I might be too late."

She walked up to him. "As long as it's now, it's not too late. It's still now, right?"

"I think so."

Her eyes widened, and she grabbed his face in her small hands, using her thumbs to gently push his eyelids closed.

When his eyes opened he was by the creek, and he was a little boy. The little blonde girl smiled, and he held a long stick in his hand, wielding it like a sword.

"Are you the princess?" asked Alex.

She nodded.

"I heard you were being held captive by dragons."

She brought a finger to her lips, telling him to be quiet. "They're hiding on the trees, all around us."

Alex held out his hand and she took it in hers. He pulled her into a run alongside the creek, jumping over it.

"Shouldn't we be sneaking?" she asked.

"They already know we're here," said Alex, turning and seeing a half-dozen bark-covered dragons dislodge from the sides of trees and fly spinning through the air at them. They were not the biggest dragons he'd seen, but there were a lot of them. He pushed the princess behind him and ran at the beasts, yelling as he ducked beneath their claws and snapping maws, lunging with his blade and piercing their bark hides. The earth shook with the force of beast after beast landing on either side of him.

More were coming from further into the trees, hearing the calls of their wounded brethren, screaming like banshees through the air.

"Princess, you know how to sword fight, right?" he asked her.

"Princesses don't know how to sword fight!"

"They learn how to fence," said Alex. "The cool ones do, anyway."

"Well, yes, of course I know how to fence! That's different."

He took his stick, cracked it in half over his knee, and tossed half to her. "There are too many. I'm going to need your help." They both braced themselves, raising their short swords as the bark-covered dragons tore through the air towards them. "Now!" yelled Alex, and they both sprinted at the evil creatures—ducking, slashing, and rolling across the dirt floor. Monster after monster fell until they stood upon a mountain of bark-covered corpses as they fought.

Alex ran and leapt over the creek, shoving his blade deep into the belly of a dragon and bringing it crashing to the ground. He put a boot on its side and yanked the sword out.

When he looked up, he saw Jamie walking up. He looked around—the princess and dragons were gone, and he was no longer a little boy.

"Alex, are you all right? You didn't say you'd be back here, I've been walking around for half an hour." She looked down at the stick he was holding and smirked. "Looks like you're feeling better. Maybe less of an asshole today?"

Alex laughed, his face twisted up—and tears began streaming down his cheeks. He dropped the stick and held the sides of his head.

"Alex!" Jamie walked up and put her arms around him, then walked him over to a log and sat him down.

"Jamie..." he said, shaking.

"Shh." Jamie held him tight. "Calm down. It's alright."

He took a deep breath and looked down at the stick on the ground. "I had a sister."

"You don't have a sister, Alex."

"Named Rachel."

"What? How come you never told me?"

"Back in upstate New York, when I was little. One day we were playing in a creek and she fell into some rocks and got hurt bad. I ran home to get help, but by the time we got back, it was too late. She had tried to get up or move and then fell into the shallow water and drowned."

"My god, Alex. I'm sorry."

"No one knows, not even Levi. I thought I was over it. But then with... when we lost the baby... it all came back." He looked into Jamie's eyes and she was crying. "I'm sorry. I had no right."

"You don't need to be sorry anymore." She hugged him tight and put her head on his shoulder. Neither one of them spoke for some time.

"I have to go away for a while," he said, finally. "I need to clear things up, open some doors."

She closed her eyes. "I'm used to being alone now."

"Just for a while."

"I can't promise that I'll be here when you get back."

"As long as you do what's best for you."

They sat there for a while, just listening to the wind and the trickling water of the creek. Eventually, it started getting dark.

"Can I walk you home?" he asked. She smiled a little, then nodded. They got to their feet, and Alex looked around at all the dragon corpses splayed out over the ground. He could smell their decaying bodies.

"You all right?" asked Jamie.

"Yeah. Yeah, I'm fine."

*   *   *

Alex walked through the dim apartment, with figures of people flashing in and out of existence around him. He fed Dora as his furniture kept vanishing and reappearing. He walked into the bathroom and looked at his face in the mirror.

In the empty apartment, he walked through the living room and up to Red, who was sitting in front of a game of Downs and Spades. The board was clear, with the pieces sitting to the side of it, and the cards were sitting in a neat stack.

"Please have a seat, Mister Sir." Red motioned to an overturned milk crate for him to sit on.

In his bathroom, he turned on the sink and splashed water onto his face.

Alex sat down across from Red. "I want to know it all. I want to be unlocked."

She passed him the deck of cards. "Your turn to deal."

Alex looked into the bathroom mirror and smiled. Then his eyes clenched shut, his body convulsed, and he fell, slamming his arm against the sink before hitting the ground.

Alex shuffled the cards and turned towards the bathroom, which no longer had furniture blocking it. The door was cracked, and the light was on.

"I hope someone takes care of Dora."

"I'm sure she'll be fine," said Red.

Alex dealt out the cards and they began playing and moving pieces.

"It might take a while," said Red. "You've stacked worlds upon worlds between you and what you want. Traversing those worlds is no hop, skip and jump. You're going to have to not be Alex for a while."

Alex placed a card down and took a piece off the board. "That sounds perfect. I wouldn't mind getting lost."

Red nodded and placed a card down. "Well, I'll have to check my calendar first, of course."

"Yes, yes, of course."

"And we'll need new names. The best part of forgetting and remembering is being able to keep changing who you are."

In the bathroom Alex lay there sprawled on the floor, blood trickling down from his nose, then dripping onto the tile.

Part III

Three men and a young girl, all four dressed in brown leather with long black coats, snuck through the thick trees and vines of the forest-covered mountain of the island. If the natives found them they'd be dead in minutes—each of them had already been wounded and they certainly couldn't live through another attack.

"Captain!" whispered the girl, peering at something ahead of them. A mass of red braids fell to her shoulders from beneath her black bandanna.

The Captain stepped up beside her, using a cutlass to push aside a few hanging vines. Amidst the trees and boulders, just before the mountain they were on dropped to become a sheer cliff, there was a shimmering blue form of a woman.

"Maybe it's related to the Temple of Goddesses," said the girl.

"It doesn't look like the statues in the temple," said the Captain. He pulled a small harpoon gun from his belt and stepped quietly towards the form. The blue woman flickered in and out of existence like a ghost, then was there again, glowing. She looked blankly forward as if she didn't see the four of them as they approached. At the woman's feet were a cluster of metal boxes, and light coming from the center of one of them.

The red-haired girl stuck her hand out into the light, and the image shivered and twisted, then was straight again. "Some kind of science," she said. "An apparition of light."

The blue woman spoke, her voice sounding rough and crackling. "I… I don't know if you can hear me, Alex. The doctor says the tumor has stopped advancing. That it's a miracle."

The Captain lowered the harpoon gun and looked up into her face. "She's beautiful," he whispered.

"They're not sure if you're gonna wake up, though…" Blue tears fell from the woman's face, and the Captain tried to catch them in vain—they vanished before reaching his gloved hand.

"She's… some sort of message carried here from another place."

"The words she's saying," said the girl, "they don't make sense. Al-ex. Too-more. Dock Tor." She pulled out an electronic device and flipped it on. A screen lit up green and it began beeping in her hand. "It might be an encryption. I'll try decoding it."

The Captain nodded, staring into the woman's blue, down-turned eyes.

Then the woman began speaking again. "I… I don't know if you can hear me, Alex. The tumor has stopped advancing…" She said the same words as before, then started crying again.

"Whoever she is," said the Captain, "I think she's important, and she needs our help." He turned to the red-haired girl. "Can you find where this signal is coming from?"

"Of course I can."

"Good. Don't worry about the encryption—just find the source. Then we'll steal a ship and get off this damned island."

The girl flipped off her device and pulled out another device, hooking it up to the metal box. "Sounds like adventure."

"What else is worth chasing?" he asked, looking once more into the blue woman's eyes. He didn't know why he felt such a strong connection to her—this stranger. "Don't worry. We're coming for you."

Insight into each
Story & Poem

the thief & the tree

Back in 2009, my friend Ariel Gratch invited me to write for an online magazine he was helping put together called The Avant Guardian. Each contributor had their own subject and published something once a week. Ariel wrote articles about performance, someone wrote about fashion, someone wrote poetry, etc.—I was there to write stories.

Mainly I wrote a series of absurd magical realism-inspired stories following the character of The Function—a strange man running around New Orleans and working for the embodiment of Serendipity, with a giant mosquito for a partner. This was the beginning of what would become my New Orleans world, the setting for my *The Agents Of* series, the first novel being *The Axeboy's Blues*.

The thief & the tree is one of the few stories I wrote for The Avant Guardian that wasn't about The Function or New Orleans, and it has always held a special place in my heart. Also, now that I read so many of my pieces on stage, I find it funny how this piece can never be read aloud, due to the missing g's and G's. Somehow that fact adds to the piece's dreaminess for me.

Flowers

I've always really loved contrast in stories and imagery, whether it's ugliness and beauty, sadness and happiness, light and darkness. I wrote *Flowers* around 2010, and I remember listening to a lot of Danny Elfman soundtracks while writing it, if that gives you an idea of my mindset at the time.

What interested me most with this story was the ugliness and metal of the machines contrasting the beauty and delicate nature of flowers. I also believe this is the only story where I've written a mad scientist type of character.

The Iris

This Dream Fragment Story was written around 2009. I created a character and their life—but instead of writing a story of them in their situation, I wrote a dream they had one night. With this particular piece, I tried to capture the shifting of place and identity inside of dreams. For a full description of my Dream Fragment Stories, see the introduction of this book.

This is the first Dream Fragment Story that I ever wrote.

Elven Creature

A piece I wrote for the stage of Esoterotica, the biweekly show in New Orleans where local authors read their original erotica and love poems. I wrote this in early 2016. I had another piece written for the show, but then I went on this crazy magical date with a lovely woman who was passing through town, and I was so inspired that I wrote this piece last minute for the show.

And yes, she was wearing a fedora. And yes, her hair was made of fire.

Compass & Ion

Another of my Dream Fragment Stories. This particular story is one which I *physically* wrote in an experimental manner. I tacked pieces of blank paper to the wall of my apartment, dressed in crazy costume attire (as one often does while living in New Orleans), along with antique welding goggles, and wrote the piece on my wall by candlelight while strange music played from my CD player.

There's a secret in the title. I didn't mean for it to be secret, thinking that some people would find it right away, but so far I have yet to have anyone find it on their own. It's really just a bit of silly wordplay—

Compass & Ion is the word *Compassion* taken apart.

One part of this story I particularly enjoy is the saxophone player, who is very inspired by Tom Waits, one of my favorite musicians.

Travels

Another piece I wrote for Esoterotica. The original version ended with me *reading* a love poem to the person instead of *writing* one, since it was written for the stage.

Travels is very influenced by magical realism, especially Italo Calvino's *Invisible Cities*—one of my favorite novels.

the girl who was the wind

Another of my Dream Fragment Stories, this one ended up being the seed for my first novel, *Spectacle of the Extension*. The novel follows Em instead of Matt. Em is a painter as well as a barista, and one night her painting comes to life, and the novel follows both her and her painting as the novel unfolds, with Matt as a side character.

The girl who was the wind is inspired by dreams that feel normal and grounded at first, but end up unraveling both visually and logically.

Ghost & the Ballroom

In the winter of 2014, the writers of Esoterotica picked each others' names randomly and wrote pieces to each other for a holiday show. I picked the amazingly talented poet Invaluable Emily and wrote this piece for her. The italicized parts were written in an attempt to reflect one of the styles which Invaluable Emily writes, and I also attempted to read them in her voice—with her tone and the way she emotes when she reads aloud. I read the non-italicized sections in a loud ringmaster voice, to create a heavy contrast between the hushed, near-whisper I used to read the italicized parts.

Two Pieces of Eight

One of my Dream Fragment Stories. The title refers to a *piece of eight*, which is an old name for the Spanish dollar, which was a silver coin in the 1600s. At one point it was common to cut the Spanish dollar into eight wedges, so two of those pieces together would be a "quarter," and the term *two pieces of eight* became synonymous with *quarter of a dollar*.

The Study

This tiny story is by far the oldest work of mine I'll ever publish. I wrote it around 2000, and I have no idea where it came from. I'm not actually certain I showed it to anyone back then, but I've always liked how haunting it is.

Age of the Moth

One of my Dream Fragment Stories. This particular story was published in an online magazine called Thieves Jargon, a website full of strange poetry and stories, which is sadly no longer around. In this story, I really tried to capture the time jumps that I experience in dreams, where I *think* about the future, and then I'm suddenly *living* a strange version of it.

Gambler's Fate

This poem I wrote in 2013, and it seems to have spawned from thinking about characters living in New Orleans in the early 1900s. I used to hang out with a lot of musicians at the time, and I became their resident poet. This was one of the pieces I would read at house concerts between musicians playing their songs. At some point, I might turn it into a longer short story, or thread it into my *The Agents Of* series.

Dame of the Eagle Saloon

Speaking of early 1900s New Orleans, this piece takes place in the same time period. The Eagle Saloon was one of the early homes to jazz music. There was a row of these saloons on Rampart Street in the Central Business District, but only a few buildings remain, abandoned and falling apart in a sea of parking lots. On the corner of Rampart and Perdido Street, the three-story building of The Eagle Saloon still stands. It's a quite magical and majestic building.

One of these old saloons, The Little Gem Saloon, was recently renovated and is now an event space and restaurant bearing the same name, which is pretty great since most of the buildings revolving around the history of jazz in New Orleans have long since vanished.

I wrote *Dame of the Eagle Saloon* in 2014 for the stage of Esoterotica, and it is published in *Enflame*, Esoterotica's 2nd Anthology.

Snake Kingdom

The last of my Dream Fragment Stories. It's also the only one that I might consider more nightmare-ish than the others. If you read a lot of my work, you'll notice that card games being played on overturned cardboard boxes by a strange set of characters is something which pops up from time to time. I do love this image. I'm in the midst of editing *The Agents Of, Volume 2*, and there is a card game on a flat section of rooftop being played by some of the main characters, one of whom is a giant mosquito— and the card game is being played on an overturned cardboard box.

Perhaps one day I'll have to write an essay on these scenes, and why I may be so drawn to them.

Dreaming Red

This story is one of my favorites, which is why I kept it for last. I actually wrote *Dreaming Red* in 2006 as a short script, and only recently rewrote it as a short story. I wrote the script while living in Seattle—I was trying to come up with inexpensive yet dreamy and magical ideas for short scripts. Since I rewrote it as a short story, I've definitely added a couple of elements which would be more expensive in script form, since I no longer had to worry about cost.

Red is a character who has come up in several of my short stories, usually as a little girl who is part of someone's subconscious, and there's a very different version of her in my debut novel, *Spectacle of the Extension*, though this story is not linked to the novel in any way.

I do hope, one day, to see this made into a short film.

Acknowledgments

A special thank you to my friends Zachary W. Mohr, Caitlyn Watson, James Smith, and JJ Kellogg for helping me edit these stories and poems—their help and friendship is immeasurable.

Thank you to Taylor Paige Amalfitano who helped edit and advise on the story Dreaming Red, helping me strengthen the story.

Also a special thanks to Corrinne Almeida, for editing help as well as coming up with the book's name and teaching me about the word "gyre."

I'd also like to thank the producers of Esoterotica, Aime' SansSavant and Shadow Angelina, for providing such a rich and wonderful environment for writers like myself to constantly challenge themselves and read their work on stage. I seriously do not know where I'd be as a writer without having been a part of Esoterotica for the last six years, in which I've written over thirty pieces and read them to live audiences.

And I'd like to thank you, reader, for taking the time to read my strange dream-stories and poetry. I hope they've inspired you in some way, whether in reality, dreams, or somewhere in between.

Zachary W. Mohr's dream-filled, amazingly illustrated fairytale books can be found at DesdemonasDreams.com

Esoterotica is a biweekly show in New Orleans featuring love poetry and erotica from local writers. Check out their anthologies and schedule at Esoterotica.com

Andy Reynolds was a gambler born in New Orleans in 1898. He lived a very messy yet deliberate life, and despite surviving numerous brushes with yellow fever, died quite young in 1936—an event involving at least one street magician, five insidious cats and a stained glass window. Three incarnations later and he again resides in New Orleans, this time as a writer of fiction and an imbiber of whiskey and local knowledge.

Find out more about his writings at: AndyReynolds.net
& also: Facebook.com/AndyWritings

Read tiny slices of his poetry: Twitter.com/AndyWritings

Watch & listen to him read poems and other such things on YouTube, on his Channel called AndyWritings.